HARDCOVERS

A lesbian mystery-romance

By

Abby Frankenstein

Table of Contents

Thanks to

My sister

Doctor Jane Frankenstein

(My Buddha)

1

Gretchen Loves, "The Character"

A blizzard brought snow, building up against the door. Gretchen did not care. Feet of snow fell as light and airy fluff, then packed down, hard as bone. Visibility was zero. Gretchen turned her back confidently and returned to make her rag dolls.

By the light of a blazing fire, she lovingly stitched the rag doll miniatures of flora and fauna, friend and foe. Absorbed in the quality of her stitches, she could leave the savage world behind, past, present, and future. She had gathered pounds of scrap cloth of hundreds of colors and textures to craft her chosen family. She worked with callused hands, performing like a surgeon. Her pudgy but nimble fingers passed the silver needles precisely, creating fine details in embroidery.

Tiny burlap arms clutched the bounties of a harvest, roses with perfect tiny pestles, polished ripe apples, bunches of purple grapes, arms full of corn, showing tiny yellow kernels or pets, kittens and chickens and pups. Each thread, chosen and picked one at a time, was woven into dimensional embellishment. Using little twigs and hay or rough string, she fashioned tools, bows and arrows, rifles, and cooking pots and baskets, some filled with ripe apples and a vegetable bouquet of carrots, beets, and corn. She spoke softly to each as she sewed them. She could trust the dolls to keep quiet if the sheriff came around. She was prepared for trouble, her 45-caliber pistol in its ornate holster.

Gretchen hummed and sang along with the wide variety of vinyl records that her father had left her twenty years ago. Murdered. She stacked several records on the stand, which gave her an hour of uninterrupted musical bliss. Gustaff Loves, father, had no time to change his mind or yank his chains; Gretchen was the only person left. She inherited all five hundred acres of the horse ranch, the impressive three-story log house, the barn, and all the tools and tractors that made it possible to maintain it. He had taught her everything she needed to know, including how to hate. A long life lived focused on hiding from hurt. Became a life of isolation.

Fire blazed yellow and bright in the wide heath of the stone fireplace. Casting Gretchen's shadow hopping along the log walls gave the impression that there were several people moving around the room. She talked to the dolls lovingly, giving them names and considering their feelings about what she included in their decorations. She heard the dolls make comments back to her; some sang, and some whistled. She would wink at them as they took on a finished level, and they winked back.

Once a week, she would load her off-road rider with things she had grown and dolls he had sewn, bounce down the back roads and buggy trails that followed the boundaries of the farms and corn fields. She wore her late father's overalls, a too-large Stetson hat, shaved her plump cheeks and chin to remove the shadow of a full beard, and two 45 caliber pistols in elaborately carved leather holsters, one on each hip. In the small town of Middlefield, the site of the odd, Gretchen Loves made an unsettling impression, and they nicknamed her "The Character."

She lived a rustic life, with no phone, little electricity, wood for heat and light at night, and a wood stove providing cooking and heat in the harshness of winter near the Great Lake of Erie. When the snow piled up, she drove her old John Deer tractor to plow the roads into her home. If a tree fell, she pulled out the chain saw and cut the thing into useable sizes, tossed them in the tractor scoop, and trundled to her stacks nearer the house to dry.

She fed and pampered her fifty chickens, tail feathers collected for her sewing use, and gathered the eggs for trade. She could not eat the flesh. They were pets and considered friends; she clucked and giggled with them, repaired her elaborate chicken coops, and delighted in their primitive conversations.

"I don't expect a long story from the hens," she mumbled to her rag dolls, "but they can tell short jokes as bright as anyone." The dolls smiled, giggled, danced on occasion, and told longer stories if they could.

She stuffed the dolls with herbs and mints that grew in her vegetable garden and around the long rows of roses her mother had planted and tended many years before.

She sniffed the herbs below her nose, inhaling deeply to interrupt the dark memories. She gathered mounds of herbs in the summer and dried them for use in the long, bitter months when the snow came. Rag dolls filled her time in the winter. She made hundreds of dolls for trade or sale, drank hot black coffee, and ate homemade chocolate chip cookies, filling the air with euphoric smells by the light of the fire.

After hours of concentrated work, she rubbed her tired eyes and put the unfinished doll in her basket, which made it cozy for the night. She chewed the last of her cookies, licked the last of the chocolate from her fingers, and tromped off to the bath.

She ran the tub full of steaming water made fragrant with bubbles, lathered up the shaving cup, mixed the soap with her brush, and then smeared the thick lather over her stubbly round cheeks and cleft chin. She drew the dead father's razor across her face with care and confidence until she was smooth.

After an hour, she dragged a heavy towel across her skin until it was dry, pulled on her long red underwear, and climbed the stairs. Pulling open the closet door, she arranged the dolls and her make-shift mattress made of her mother's old coats, checked the shot gun's loaded ammunition, tucked it under her pillow made of her mother's old dresses, closed the door, and went to sleep.

2

Rose Cox spelunks her skull.

Dream-spelunking between the cap of her skull and the matter of her brains, Rose Cox imagined she was crawling through mysterious ruts, squeezing, naked, shoulder-deep through the tight, slippery turns of thinking flesh. Serpentine, smart muscle, packed like spongy mounds of chewed bubble gum, squeaked against her skin as she searched for the hot spots, the nerve origins of her migraines.

She ducked under the greasy texture of cranial bone. Sparks from working neurons lit her way like the strobe lights in a spinning, mirrored disco ball. She felt blood pulsate through tissue, tough and pink. Undulating like an eel, pressing out and down with her knees, she oozed through the maze. Curling her fingertips, she clung to jagged sutures joining her skull plates, dragging herself along. She was getting closer to the pain. Strangely, it tickled.

As she wriggled, she rolled over pressure points that released tension like a masseur's therapeutic knuckles pressing into a knotted muscle, smoothing anxiety. Tracking the pain growing in her optic nerves, she considered this torture might be deserved purgatory for her sins.

The inside of her skull was beautiful. The bone ceiling, tan and alive, had the texture and temperature of hot beach sand. She traced the zig-zag seams in her skull with her finger, comforting herself and focusing on the lovely things she gave up after getting sick and being fired.

Finally, locating the hot spot of pain behind her eye, she envisioned grinding a rod of ice into the suffering nerve, envisioning it frozen solid, paralyzed, terminating the throbbing.

"Right there, only there," she meditated, taking control of the agonized point. "Right there, one moment at a time."

She prayed daily to God for forgiveness and guidance through the worst time of her life, but she feared she had been abandoned. No answer.

Her eyes rolled under gritty lids. Tears welled up in response to the drag of her eyeballs along the dryness. Tears came, and her eyes welcomed the wetness that seeped into the micro-space between her swollen lids and her bloodshot eyes.

"The pills are wearing off," thought Rose. Her aching pelvis was a warning; it must be morning.

The pain behind her eyes was growing sharper in spite of her meditation. She panicked. Soon, she would be wide awake. She quickened her pace needed to visit the art gallery, her dome of art. For traction, her toes curled and dipped into the lush lining. Finally, she was there, comforted by the images.

Simple line drawings that had hung in her old office appeared on the bone above her, colorful and bouncing like animated cartoons. Familiar illustrations, originally scratched onto paper with crayons, greeted her. Lustrous reminders of friends drove her deep into her interior and begged her to stay until she woke. They reminded her of being warm and loved.

The artwork, drawn by adults with unique minds, depicted abstract bodies: some shaped like a potato, torsos with crooked legs, running on bulbous feet with sticks for arms, simple circles for faces, jagged squares for teeth, four eyes or no eyes or just a mouth. Impressionistic scribbles and colors scattered in her memory. Dreams of days when she felt alive rolled like a silent movie, sensitive and private. She loved the direct quality of the art, like the exquisite prehistoric cave drawings left by ancient people, depicting animals in their rugged lives. These pictures showed the pieces of her life and lost career.

Unset alarm clock buttons collected dust after months of Rose sleeping until noon or until she could not stand the aching anymore. Prescription pain pills rolled around on the crowded bedside stand among crumpled tissues and an ashtray full of butts. The childproof bottles remained uncapped; tops were hurled into the trash out of frustration when it took pliers to get them open. She had to be able to give herself pills, at least!

"My God! Am I that pathetic that a pill bottle could overwhelm me?" she thought.

The darkness of the bedroom felt like a coffin lid, crushing her, suffocating her. Trembling and wrestling with shame, each morning spiraled into a murky depression. Another morning was a dread.

Sleep protected her briefly from the daily slog around the kitchen, hunting through lean cupboards. No longer humming while she cooked. She cringed at the sight of unpaid bills, tight in their envelopes, in a growing stack on the table. An ever increasing mound of bills toppled over, spilling onto the male and female Pilgrim salt and pepper shakers, still dressing the table from last Thanksgiving. The last party she had given before the crap hit the fan.

The couple seemed to mock her long sleep habits by laying sideways on the table. Their cocky, painted grins and placid expressions on ruddy faces contrasted her grim reality. The little judges folded their arms in traditional black and white costumes and stared back at her while clutching colorful cornucopias of inedible ceramic bounty while grains of salt and pepper sprinkled from their perfect little head holes.

"Perfect little Christians," she thought.

Rose was growing to hate them and felt guilty for it. She had envisioned herself saved, morally correct, representing right, earning respect by hard work and earnest love of God, straight and clean. A life spent following the rules seemed to have been unappreciated by God. Now, she found herself begging in her prayers for the divine forgiveness she thought she already had. Did her transgressions warrant the purgatory called cancer?

Rose had prided herself on her good reputation, solid ethics, and excellent credit. Now, she worried she would be buried in debt and die crippled. She made a bitter discovery: that if you question power, you pay the price, even working in a humane social service agency like Adult Action Services.

Blood trickled from her into the super-absorbent pad she had to put on or wander in pools of blood. Her cramps bit in. She fought back by conjuring images of client faces. The rewards of working at the sheltered workshop were not appreciated by everybody. It took special patience to get into the rhythm, empathize with the disappointments, and celebrate the victories.

She recalled satisfaction supporting the strengths of other-abled workers as they met the daily challenges. The sharp change from gladness to shame descended when the old boss's jowly face came into view. Ken Musk's imagined presence curdled her dream life just as his actual presence had in her work life. Her throat tightened.

It jangled her nerves to recall how she had been ambushed by Ken's invitation to a private meeting that became a grope fest early in her employment at A.A.S. She had worn long sleeves to cover the bruises he left that summer. She stayed because she needed a paycheck, and he had given her a raise for her inconvenience and her silence. Money convinced her to go against what she knew was right.

She never reported him. He bought her like a whore. She admitted to herself in disgrace.

She had carefully designed methods to avoid being alone with the "Silver Fox" again, or as her best friend and coworker, Oceanna Pontiac had called him, "Gray Frog," referring to his balding head, bulging eyes, and toad-shaped body.

"I gave in," she whispered. Chapped lips ground against each other with each small movement, tearing short flaps of dry skin as the upper and lower scraped along. Her prayers for forgiveness fell flat, and her crimes continued to cling. "Forgive me," she begged silently into the sheet covering her face.

Snorting through tight sinuses, she stirred, turning her face to the clock, flashing a red twelve. That, and the slowly reheating electric heating pad under her hips, told her the power had been off for a while and just come back on. The wind gusted outside her window. Through the gap in the curtain, she could see thick ice forming as sleet pelted down, crackling against the roof like gravel. Oregon's infamous silver thaw storms could seal Portland in under inches of ice for days.

Freezing rainstorms occasionally overtook the Northwest. The temperatures would drop, and the rain would fall from the sky as a liquid, becoming ice the moment it hit land. Inches of ice would build up one drop of rain after the other, creating a crystal-clear sheet encasing everything. The city would become paralyzed, shimmering under the added weight of millions of pounds of ice on every branch, roof, and street power line, tearing them down. Rose considered her luck; this time, she wouldn't have to chip her car out to go to work.

It jangled her nerves to recall how she had been ambushed by Ken's invitation to a private meeting that became a grope fest early in her employment at A.A.S. She had worn long sleeves to cover the bruises he left that summer. She stayed because she needed a paycheck, and he had given her a raise for her inconvenience and her silence. Money convinced her to go against what she knew was right. She never reported him. He bought her like a whore. She admitted to herself in disgrace.

She had carefully designed methods to avoid being alone with the "Silver Fox" again, or as her best friend and coworker, Oceanna Pontiac had called him, "Gray Frog," referring to his balding head, bulging eyes, and toad-shaped body.

"I gave in," she whispered. Chapped lips ground against each other with each small movement, tearing short flaps of dry skin as the upper and lower scraped along. Her prayers for forgiveness fell flat, and her crimes continued to cling. "Forgive me," she begged silently into the sheet covering her face.

Snorting through tight sinuses, she stirred, turning her face to the clock, flashing a red twelve. That, and the slowly reheating electric heating pad under her hips, told her the power had been off for a while and just come back on. The wind gusted outside her window. Through the gap in the curtain, she could see thick ice forming as sleet pelted down, crackling against the roof like gravel. Oregon's infamous silver thaw storms could seal Portland in under inches of ice for days.

Freezing rainstorms occasionally overtook the Northwest. The temperatures would drop, and the rain would fall from the sky as a liquid, becoming ice the moment it hit land. Inches of ice would build up one drop of rain after the other, creating a crystal-clear sheet encasing everything. The city would become paralyzed, shimmering under the added weight of millions of pounds of ice on every branch, roof, and street power line, tearing them down. Rose considered her luck; this time, she wouldn't have to chip her car out to go to work.

At the center of the event, toiling in the smoke and meat, was Oceanna Pontiac, long silver tongs in her hands, sweating over the stainless-steel grill, hot dogs and burgers sizzling. Her short blond hair was tied hurriedly into two short pigtails that stuck out unevenly over each ear. Smiling broadly, she plopped meat into waiting buns, many of them piled extra deep with relish and ketchup, onions, and chili. The gang of hungry workers squeezed in tight, seeking another helping, jostling Oceanna, who laughed and made jokes to welcome them in.

Recalling her friend enjoying the closeness of her clients and comrades tugged at Rose's heart, charming her into a deep appreciation for Oceanna's capacity to give. Ken had called Oceanna a "bull dagger," accusing all lesbians of wife stealing, warning Rose against becoming friends because of the risks of exposure to "what those perverts were really after." She had been drawn to her naturally, in spite of the warnings, and was glad for it.

Then, she recalled watching Ken's perverted eye scan over the back side of a teenager at the barbecue. A pubescent girl in a tight tank top, revealing female charms, bare arms, and a tan back, reminded her of the level of his vulgarity and the reason for her disgust.

Rose felt nauseated recalling Ken entertaining a circle of female office workers, chatting in low-cut blouses, brown chests embellished with thin gold chains, dangling little gold crucifixes intended to tumble in and out of cleavage, rigged to tease the boss while they mocked and rolled their eyes behind his back.

Ken Musk was taking a second run at youth, sporting a dyed comb-over, a paunch rolling over his belt, a horizontally striped shirt, baggy golf shorts, and expensive cars, making him look frumpy and comedic.

His dirty money gave him power, making obedience the only route to self-preservation, Rose thought.

Curling in on herself, Rose took a mental stroll through the old warehouse workshop. A highly curved Quonset warehouse, several blocks long with a corrugated metal roof, created a continuous open space. The arched roof rebounded with every sound. The cacophony invigorates the work atmosphere. The noise of forklift horns, ringing phones, hammers banging, and voices calling out was satisfying evidence of empowerment.

Shuttle drivers called passengers' names over loudspeakers hourly when vans came to pick up and drop off workers. As part of their disability benefits, buses transported workers with a wide variety of disabilities, physical and mental, defined as "other-abled," to job sites all over town.

Light manufacturing and packaging projects were done by workers with simpler skill sets and less training. Hundreds of jobs requiring long hours of repetitive, small steps readying products for the market required people seeking the same.

Folks who could not manage the tricks and details of that particular day's assembly line project waited at community tables, sat with friends, and chatted or drew pictures to take home. What at first glance seemed crude, simple drawings became precious gifts to Rose and Oceanna.

Rose smiled, "The place was always such a mess. Watching the clients with wheelchairs and canes try to rock and limp over electric cords and old cardboard was a nightmare."

She wondered how anyone found their way out of their workstations. The boxes of products were piled so high that people couldn't see over them. Their hands were blackened from grime on the floor sticking to their wheels as they rolled over dust to their workstations on the long cement floor.

However dysfunctional or dirty, it was their shop, their job. They took home earned money, paid at piece rate, according to their counts of the number of chocolate-covered coffee beans packaged or snow boots labeled and tagged, the number of muffler gaskets tied to cardboard disks and shrink-wrapped, cartons of greeting cards boxed, crates of flag poles varnished, or the number of bundles of newspaper coupons collated and stuffed, or pounds of red and brown cat kibble sealed up into bright bags and more.

Every day brought new contracts, large and small, that was fun. Every day, the population of workers trundled off the buses, indiscreetly labeled with large letters announcing "Transportation for the Developmentally Disabled" on three sides. Five days a week, vans rolled up, clients disembarked, streamed in, and participated in their pieces of the American dream. Their enthusiasm and determination were inspirations.

The short buses became a distinct part of the neighborhoods they trundled down, mornings and afternoons. The drivers blocked the narrow streets, warning bells ringing, beeping, lights flashing, signaling riders climbing off. Some use the front steps, and others require the deployment of electric lifts and ramps to give wheelchair riders a way out and in.

Many evenings after work, Oceanna and Rose devoured green apple martinis and appetizers at bohemian bars while they laughed and cried, sharing human stories. They discovered they were kindred spirits, leaning into each other for support and becoming closer than the social work sisters they started out as. The boundaries of their relationship evaporated as they shared their connections with others.

Rose's prim social rules had been useful in keeping Ken at bay. He had gazed dreamily at her across the boardroom, wore pants too tight in the right places, and positioned his manhood, hoping to lure her into noticing his hard lap. He had accidentally, but on purpose, rubbed his palms across her back while in a tight crowd. She shuddered at the lewd memory.

Ken could not give up on trying to trap her, creating some masculine pressure; anything to get laid was fine with him. Adding to the catastrophe was his sad, humiliated wife, who was aware he was cheating. She was reduced to public breakdowns, pleading for attention during company parties, the evenings ending with her going home in a cab alone and sobbing. She apologized for such spectacles at his request. Ken manipulated the situation to get sympathy sex from his intimidated employees. He called himself a politician, but Rose considered him a vulgar beast devouring low-hanging fruit like herself. Nausea accompanied the thought.

Oceanna remarked that she thought the greedy bastard was trying to kill her by breaking her spirit. In church, Rose listened to the minister give sermons about men picking up on the unclean thoughts exuded from lustful women's hearts and subtle messages in body language. Rose questioned herself: was she guilty of this sin? The internal inquisition rolled frequently in her mind because she had lustful thoughts, but not about Ken.

Oceanna called it bullshit. Rose was beautiful, that was all. The sight of her curvaceous shape scurrying down the hall, dress clinging to some parts and billowing around others, compelled admiration. Innocence seemed to envelop her. Images of Rose in daily life remained vivid in Oceanna's mind.

Rose was blond, pale, well-built, and simply unoccupied with it. She made cunning jokes, stunning people with robust laughter, and she had a spark that flashed in her pale gray eyes. The most attractive quality was that Rose was genuine.

Oceanna spied Ken's growing anxiety at the thought of coming in second to an aging dyke, ten years older than Rose, with short, cropped hair and skin decorated with dragon and mermaid tattoos.

Rose held a guilty pleasure imagining that Ken might be in pain over their friendship.

"Heroes in the trenches, fighting a common enemy, perhaps," Rose thought.

The morning's freezing gale drove down sheets of rain that turned to ice, glazing the roof and rattling the windows. Heaving a sigh, she braced to face another day of isolation. She had little money or energy to confront a winter morning with any oomph. But she had to get up and take care of her leaks and bring up her levels of caffeine, nicotine, and Oxycodone.

Rose pulled her knees up to her chest and, on the count of "one, two, three," hoisted herself up on her torso, then onto her elbows, and spun slowly to work her feet over the edge of the bed. Lowering her legs slowly, she set her feet on the chilly wood floor. She snatched a palm full of pain pills and swallowed them dry, rocked forward, putting weight on her tiptoes, bent forty-five degrees at the waist, and padded into the bathroom to clean it all up.

Half awake, she labored to clean up and place a fresh, huge menstrual pad in her panties, intended for after birth. The doctor's appointment was this week, both a relief and a burden; at least she would find out what was happening to her.

While in the bathroom, the phone rang, and a message was in the process of being recorded. It was Oceanna with her daily encouragement call.

3
Hello Oceanna.

"Hello, Rose, it's Oceanna! I know you're there, Rosy Cox. I know you're hang-dog and sore, but it is time to take control! Stand up! Get up, Rose, and take the day. Drag up and get moving. Maybe dance? Dance and shake to Elvis or just for the hell of it, but move, girl, move! If you do not pick up, I'll sing. Are you ready? Ok, here we go…"

"Stop! Please… stop, I am here!" Rose snatched the phone up with her free hand and grabbed a pack of menthols with the other, spun slowly, and landed her sore hips into the recliner, then hauled an overstuffed, multicolored crazy quilt over her legs and tucked her feet under her hips.

"You're panting," said Oceanna.

"I kind of ran," Rose sucked on the filter while putting fire to the smoke.

"It sounds like panting," said Oceanna.

"To dyke's ears maybe, but it's smoking, I'm ashamed to say," she pushed some of the butts to the side of the small glass ashtray, making room for fresh ash.

"Well, this sounds hopeful. You're doing something like running and smoking. That's better than remaining in a coma," said Oceanna, smiling.

"Six of one, half dozen of another . . .," Rose winced, shifting in her chair.

"Let's change the subject. What are you wearing?" Oceanna grinned.

"Oh, a two-foot-wide menstrual pad and the crazy quilt clients made me," she sucked on her smoke eagerly.

Another arctic blast rattled the windows near the recliner, causing ice pellets to scatter across the glass and making the building thicker. Undulating shadows of the electric wires outside swung back and forth across the living room. The streetlights flickered on and off and on. Rose lit a candle.

"Sexy! Oh, hang on a second," said Oceanna.

Rose heard a clamber in the background. Oceanna could be heard in the distance, in the kitchen, talking to her father.

"Dad . . . just drink a cup of coffee. I will be there in a minute. I'm talking to Rose Cox back in Oregon. I'll make eggs in a minute if you spill a little, so what? Just stay in your chair before you fall down again. The TV is on the weather channel. You like it, right."

She came back to the phone and took a slurp of coffee, "What time you got there?"

"I Don't know the power went out. It must be about 6 a.m. I wish I had coffee. Wow, I miss you," she sighed, watching the candle flicker.

"Ya, I miss you too. It's been a bad year. The crash took most of the money I had! Dad and I went belly up about this time last year. Happy New Year, by the way."

Oceanna watched her father lift his mug with a shaky hand. He pursed his lips and stuck his neck out. He trembled the cup to his face, trying to get his mouth around the coffee before he soiled his favorite robe while staring at the production credits for the latest tornado documentary.

"I hear the ice hitting the house. Is it a bad one?" she remarked.

"You've got to love the Columbia Gorge. It brings pleasure and pain." Rose craved coffee of her own enough to slide gingerly to the edge of the seat and stand up. "I hope I can still get to the doctor's assessment this week. They're going to tell me something, I hope. The bleeding is getting worse, and the pain is constant."

Shuffling her feet across the floor, holding the phone under her chin, she loaded the coffee maker and watched it spit steam into the grounds.

"Rose, you have got to make it to the doctor. I can't take care of both of you from Ohio. Can you take a cab? I'll send you money as soon as I can. I don't take no for an answer! How are you managing your head? Praying and journaling still, I hope. All this drama would make an intense book," pleaded Oceanna.

"I can take the train," Rose mumbled to herself, "I distract myself by watching bunches of detective shows, and I still have my journals."

She glanced at the flashy covers of her detective mystery magazines as she passed her coffee table on her way to the recliner.

"Hey, speaking of distractions, I saw a talk show about a young gal who had no writing experience and wrote a novel after she had given birth. She said she was confined at home because she couldn't afford a babysitter. So, she ends up writing this great novel right there and then, with the newborn on her lap. Her first book is a bestseller! We should do something like that!" She lowered her body slowly into the recliner, took a sip of coffee, and lit another smoke.

"Hey, Rose, that's not bad. You're the one who told me about that article in your magazine talking about organizing a story, writing a paragraph for each chapter, or something until the entire book is outlined, and then you go back and fill it out with the details. We can do that, maybe? God knows we have the time right now. Hey, this may be what we need! Writing is good therapy." Oceanna hoped to be helpful, "Let's face it, we need some kind of help."

Oceanna licked the paper of the hand-rolled cigarette she was shaping, placed the narrow end in her lips, struck a stick match on the iron wood stove, and lit it. A few orange sparks drifted up from the side door as she stoked it with another bit of branch.

"We've talked about writing something; that's what everybody says, though," said Rose.

The heat from the coffee penetrated Rose's cup, passing the warmth to her skin and stinging her palms. She turned the mug around, settling on the handle for a good grip as she considered the actual task of writing any kind of long story. She tested her feelings about sharing her burdens through a novel. Maybe she is taking her anger out on a deserving boss or two.

"Hmm. I do kind of like this idea. You must write one too then. You want to join me in a therapeutic adventure?" said Rose

"Hell, Ya! I think it's great! We could have fun and… dare I say… sell?" Oceanna rolled the idea over in her mind. "I'm putting a lot of sex in mine! The way I like it… I never see that in books."

Dad tipped over his TV tray while trying to put down his mug. His robe sleeve caught on the edge, sending the mug and Kleenex to scatter across the floor.

"Rose, I gotta Go. Dad's tearing down the house! Instructions for the week: get to the doctor, take care of yourself, and think about a story to write. I'll call soon. By-by!" The receiver clattered down on the cradle and went silent.

Rose sat smoking in the candlelight with the dead phone in her ear, considering the possibility of writing down her experience, her friend's soft voice playing over in her head.

The candle flickered as though responding to Rose's thoughts. She felt a calm come over her and sensed being joined by something spiritual. Another blast of howling wind and ice hit her roof and finally overburdened the power lines, ripping them free and cutting the lights off from her house down to five blocks beyond hers. The cover of one of her magazines fluttered, turning to a particular page. The candle flame flared higher, glowing gold, illuminating the title of the magazine cover that included the article about how to write a mystery novel that they had discussed.

For the first time in a good long time, Rose felt prompted, connected, nudged. "An answer!" she thought.

How would it feel to deliver justice in her own way, she wondered? What would it be like working out the way the good guys win? She laughed, and tears trickled down her cold cheeks as she sat in the dark. She considered the possibilities. A tiny spark of hope popped into her mind. She felt a lift.

"At least I could control the characters in a story," she thought.

Her curiosity flashed on the guilty pleasure of discovering what Oceanna meant by writing about sex the way she liked it, then she flipped to the pages of the inspiring article, lit a smoke, and leaned nearer the candlelight to read about how to get started delivering justice between a couple of hardcovers.

4

Time Bomb

Jack Pontiac felt trapped. He woke up confused. Unsure if he was dreaming or really racing along behind a fire truck, careening to another thousand-acre grass fire. The memory was nothing new but never got old. Jack Pontiac was thrilled working as a news photographer, dashing over smoke-choked roads to another desperate calamity. Storming into another San Bernardino cul-de-sac and going up in a brush fire was a privilege.

He felt feverish. Sticky with sweat and wet with urine, clutching the bed rails, he rattled them madly. "Fire! Fire!" he cried.

His vision was murky in low light, but he managed to make out the lamp and the bed stand and animal prints on his sheets. They looked like camping scenes with horned moose grazing on a background of green flannel, the sheets now wadded up and tangling around his feet. "Alaska outback," he grumbled.

Trembling fingers fumbled over the plastic adult diapers, enveloping him below the navel. He picked at the plastic edges to scratch his groin, making the itch worse. Body oils left brown wax under his fingernails. "Fire! Nurse! I... need a nurse!" he wheezed in a voice slightly above a dry whisper. "I need a pot, damn it!"

"I've got you, Dad," a familiar voice called back from the yellow-lighted hall.

"In here! I'm in here!" He rolled on his side and peered over the sheets and rails, panting. Shadows on the wall indicated she was heading his way. A rush of uncertainty gripped him. He pulled the sheets over his nose and held his breath. A silhouette entered the room and approached his bed.

"Come on, Dad. It's time to get up and shower." The female moved to the nightstand, clanked a few pill bottles, and pulled a few drawers.

"Who is it? Is that you?" Dad mumbled.

"It's Oceanna, your daughter, remember?"

"Oh, Ya," Dad slowly recalled where he was. An old memory came to mind of a light-haired little girl playing on a beach wearing an oversized rubber bathing cap sprinkled with rubber flowers. She held a red shovel and patted wet sand into a bucket while splashing on the shore of the Pacific Ocean that washed over her tanned, pudgy legs.

She squinted up at him leaning over her, the California sun glaring down from behind his head in a clear blue sky. The toddler looked up into the sky through little, unbreakable dark green glasses, grinning at her dad as he snapped photos of her.

He appreciated the rhythmic buzz-click noise of the camera's mechanisms. Repeatedly, he recollected the soothing sound of the mechanical shutter. The familiar weight of the body of the Pentax 1000 in his hands brought him peace. He wished to feel the velvet glide of the lens rings as he focused perfectly, tightly framing the objects in front of him.

"Come on, Dad, Happy New Year morning," she sighed, tugging at the sheets, "Dad, it's Oceanna, and it's time to get up and start the day. Are you all right?"

Oceanna peeled his fingers from the sheets and put her face closer to her father's furrowed brow. She lifted away the sheets, exposing a bald head containing two murky blue eyes and a spotted scalp with several spoon-sized divots, sore but healing after skin cancers had been frozen away.

She thought her father looked like the quintessential octogenarian, with all the failing parts and pieces. The quintessential aging man, liver-spotted skin, a crook nose that dripped, dimming vision, trembling hands, stooped shoulders, adult diapers, diabetes, curmudgeonly spirit, and an increasingly vacant memory. He had hit every feeble step on his way up to ninety. Increasing feebleness required Oceanna to come as the obligated caregiver.

Oceanna was considered by Dad to hold fewer talents than her older sister. Therefore, she expected to drop her life and take care of him after her mother's death, triggering his increased drinking and downward spiral into dysfunction.

Attempting to surmount the emotional strain, father and daughter worked the best they could to keep him comfortable and build a functional, albeit clumsy, bond.

Jack Pontiac had never wanted children. A point he had announced in drunken episodes to his children many times. Her mother explained that Dad was "too smart and too selfish to be kind." Ironically, the only thing he had retained in full, at this point, was his selfishness.

"It's time to get up and take pills and shower. Let's go," she grinned at him, hoping to engage some enthusiasm, at least for sitting up. She leaned over him and lifted his stiff arm around her neck, slid one arm around his back and one hand under his bony knees, counted to three to get him ready to assist, and swung him to a seated position in one fluid move. His red legs got goose-bumped as they dangled over the edge of the bed like a child, feet twitching.

"Elise was in my dream; we were on the beach on a sunny day," Dad whispered.

"She was beautiful like that. Sunbathed and free." He whimpered and started to tear up.

"I miss her too. She left us while she was anticipating a good party, though. What could be better than passing in your sleep looking forward to a party?" Oceanna said, "She had that big pile of Easter eggs she intended to hide for me to hunt, but I couldn't find them!" She put slippers on his feet, "You did good by her, Dad."

She hugged him for a little cry, wiped his nose, and then assisted Dad to slide forward so he could press down on the balls of his feet. He carefully planted them on the floor. Pulling the walker over, he leaned forward and held on to the gray handles. She guided his robe on over one hand at a time and tied the belt in a knot to prevent getting tangled up, freeing him to put one foot in front of the other, squeaking his way to the bathroom.

"What about Juanita?" He looked up at her from a hunched stance, "Where is she?"

"Sis is a counselor sobering up movie stars in L.A. Wanna go?" She waited for some sign of recognition.

"Juanita fixes movie stars?" He thought a moment, "Oh Ya," he nodded, "That's my girl."

He pointed to the faded color print of an old 8 X 10 glossy of Oceanna, about ten years old, and Juanita, five years her senior, posing on a huge bolder that was part of a mile-long breakwater stretching out into the glistening Redondo Beach Harbor. The Pacific waves, long and roiling below their feet. Oceanna sported her favorite shirt with a blue whale, while Juanita wore tight paisley print bell bottoms and a gauzy blouse rippling in the breeze, looking like her hero, Janice Joplin.

The summer sun glinted off of their long, windblown hair. Expressions were mysterious. The girls' faces, though smiling, suggested sadness. Juanita focused a long gaze out to sea, too contemplative and grim for a girl of fifteen. At the same time, Oceanna smiled broadly at her sister with slightly open lips and questions in her eyes.

Dad took the picture, standing out of the scene, balancing dangerously on rocks covered with sharp barnacles, chewing at his deck shoes with waves rolling at his heels. The master records life at a comfortable distance through glass lenses and aluminum boxes lined with mirrors and shudders, recording moments elegantly.

Dad masked his discomfort with human beings by covering his face with a camera. His art provides a safe vehicle for necessary connections. Photographs were his best evidence that he was matched up with family and friends. Pictures were things he could point at proving his attachments, immortalizing them in the language of black and white. He brought out the best and the worst in his subjects, creating a reputation for which he became famous and infamous.

"Now, can we get to the bathroom before you poop your pants, old man?" Oceanna put her arms around his waist, bracing her legs in a wide stance.

"Too late!" Dad laughed out loud. They pulled him up on the count of 'one, two, three' and began a slow trudge, clanking his way to the tub.

After his bath and devouring a meal of fresh eggs and pancakes smothered in real maple syrup, Dad slept through a Browns game while Oceanna cleaned the kitchen and his room and laundered the sheets, blankets, and towels.

She made lists of needed items, examining the shelves for numbers of pills and quantity of adult diapers and over-the-counter remedies, making sure they were well stocked. She compulsively organized them for any eventuality after the first chaotic week when she received the alarming call that he was in the hospital. She swooped to Ohio to help him.

She had sped across the forty-eight states in three days, speeding from Portland, Oregon to Montville, Ohio, to find Dad in a deteriorated state, crying in a soiled bed, in an Urgent Care facility, begging to be taken home. His black and blue nose and cheek scraped from tumbling down the stairs after drinking heavily alone at home.

It was a miracle he was found alive by his Amish carpenter, who happened to come by to see if the new septic tank was operating properly. The robust and ruddy Mr. Burkholder, along with his wife and five children, had become friends after he had spent years refinishing miles of woodwork, roofing, and remodeling on the centennial farmhouse they retreated to after retiring.

The ambulance ride back was a blur of flashing lights, sirens, and the smell of antiseptic. Dad, surprisingly, enjoyed the ride. He sat bolt upright, eyes wide with a mischievous glint, watching the world whiz by. He felt like a celebrity, a fugitive from justice.

"Faster! Go faster!" he yelled to the driver.

Oceanna, exhausted and exhilarated, held his hand, feeling a surge of fierce protectiveness and a strange sense of liberation. They were running away from something, breaking free from the sterile, suffocating environment of the hospital.

Back at the farm, she settled him into his own room, overlooking the orchard, the scent of damp earth and apple blossoms filling the air. The room was filled with fading photographs and relics of a life lived. Pictures of Elise, young and vibrant, smiling radiantly. Pictures of himself, younger, leaner, with a mischievous glint in his eye, holding a camera.

He looked around the room, a flicker of recognition in his eyes. "Home," he whispered, a tear rolling down his cheek.

Oceanna knew then that bringing him home was the right decision. It might not be easy, but it would be his home, surrounded by the ghosts of his past, the echoes of his life, and the love of his daughter.

As he drifted off to sleep, a faint smile touched his lips. He dreamt of Elise, laughing, her hair flying in the wind, running through a field of wildflowers. And for the first time in a long time, he felt a sense of peace.

A female emergency technician recognized him from the number of times he had shown up, unofficially, with his cameras to house fires and car crashes in the Ohio countryside, covering emergencies even after he retired. He beamed at her, called her by name, and took her hand to thank her.

As they made their escape that night, Oceanna pursued the ambulance, keeping pace as they sped. With emergency lights flashing and sirens blaring over the entire trip home, along rolling country roads, under a blanket of shimmering stars and a bright crescent moon, they chatted. She watched Dad and the nurse through the rear windows of the ambulance. As the nurse comforted him, they discussed the latest body count and the latest bloody event that had struck the locals. Dad inquired about the gruesome details with a glimmer in his eyes, grinning and laughing as the thrill of a fast-paced ride shook him from depression.

Oceanna sighed and shook her head, continuing to fold the sheets, reminiscing about the colorful social life left behind in Portland. She was haunted by her old career, home, parties, wet weather, and women, all sacrificed to dote on her miserable old man.

She stuffed the flannel sheets into the old pine dresser at the end of Dad's bed, chose sheets with a bass fishing theme, and dressed the hospital bed. After lowering the mattress to the level of Dad's knees for the next nap time, she rolled it back into place, set out his next round of noon pills in a paper cup, peeked into the living room to see Dad, feet up in his recliner, snoring with his chin resting on his chest and headed into the kitchen for another cup of thick black coffee and a break.

Snow blew horizontally as January brought in another storm. Snow piled up at the windows on the west side to the sills. She wished she had hauled more wood in during the last easing, but there was enough to go for a few more hours if she had to. Oceanna kept the house hot for Dad.

Flipping the channels, she stopped at the national news when she thought she heard the family name. Quickly turning up the volume, I saw a story about the new freedom of speech museum called the "Newseum," opening in Washington, DC. The main exhibit was being assembled as a tribute to Pulitzer Prize-winning news photos, presenting the Pulitzer Prize winners from every year, starting from the first in the 1940s, including Dad's in the '50s.

"Dad, wake up! You're on TV! Look, it's your winner, gonna go in the Newseum!" she shook his shoulder, "Wake up!"

5

Wake up, Dad, You're on TV!

ad lifted his head upon hearing his name, just in time to see his prize winner flashed on the screen. A following series of flattering shots of a younger, more nimble Jack Pontiac, leaping over rows of fire hoses, camera in hand, confident expression, running in the direction of another emergency in his prime, followed.

He brightened, smiling a yellow smile. "Well, how about that? It's about time," he remarked, putting up one middle finger in a defiant gesture. "Make me a martini to celebrate, dear! Make it a double. Join me?"

Vodka martinis looked more glamorous in the long-stemmed glasses, but Dad had the tremors, so Oceanna poured the vodka into stout crystal tumblers and soaked Queen-sized green olives on long plastic swords for vegetables. Elise used to joke that when out at dinner parties, after getting so lubricated prior to the main course arriving, she could not eat. She would eat the cocktail garnishes, proudly stating, "I have consumed my vegetables for the day before passing out."

Dad stirred his drink as it sat on the TV tray. Oceanna clinked glasses in congratulations.

"Well, no rest for the wicked, Father. How does it feel to be immortal?" she savored a gulp of the smooth, clear drink and smacked her lips.

Dad dropped a straw into his glass, tightened his thin lips over the end of the straw, flexed his cheeks, and sucked up the elixir like an old hummingbird inserting its long snout at a feeder. He stared at the television. After draining his glass, he aimed the olive-filled sword into his jaw and plucked one olive at a time off the skewer, chewing it vigorously until all were gone. Then he lifted the empty glass in her direction as a silent request for a second, never turning his head or taking his eyes off the screen.

"Perfect!" he mumbled.

Setting down the second martini with a fresh "Happy New Year" napkin, she asked, "What's the secret, Dad?" She looked up at the grainy print in a humble wooden frame above the mantle. "This simple picture won over every other shot taken that year?" she said. "Seriously, this shot, a man and a woman struggling on a beach, was the most outstanding story?"

Dad didn't turn from the screen showing the latest weather report.

"Of all the news coverage, among all shots that must have been taken that year. I have always wondered what it is with this one?" she puzzled.

He continued to gaze hypnotically at the TV, holding the olive skewer close to his lips.

"It's what's not seen . . . the ticking time bomb," he said flatly and grabbed another olive with pursed lips, sucking the alcohol from it. A thin rivulet of vodka trickled from the skewer to his shaking fingers, down his thumb to his wrist, and along his forearm into the cuff of his bathrobe.

Oceanna watched him and sipped her drink, waiting for wisdom. Finally, she plucked the remote from the arm of his chair and turned off the set in frustration. "Dad! Really, what is it? Tell me again, what is the secret?" She could see the drink was loosening him up and thought there might be some interesting discussion due to it. She tapped him on the hand holding the straw.

"More drinks!" he blustered but did not look at her.

"Okay, more drinks after the story of the missing things and the ticking bombs. What about um?" Oceanna sat still, indicating to Dad that the vodka was not going to appear if he didn't share.

He looked up at the picture that had changed his life and took several moments to recall the details of the tragic situation that would have passed with little notice had the stars not aligned in his favor that day. He recalled getting the call that an emergency was in progress over the lifeguard radio. He recalled the power of the storm on the beach half a block away from his beach home. Having pulled on his official red trunks and embroidered lifeguard badge on the hip, he ran up the shore and spotted people struggling on the sand near storm surge waves. He snapped a shot of the anguish on the couple's faces, unsure of what had happened. Newsman's instincts kicked in; he had raised the camera at precisely the right time, held a firm stance and his breath, and clicked the shutter, making himself a news photographer's celebrity. He recalled the layers of grief and gladness that tortured him for years after benefiting from their anguish.

"It's the tension on their faces, look," he pointed a brown fingernail at the print. "You see their confusion, hopelessness. You don't need to know what's after them, but you're left wondering what's happened or what's going to happen." He looked at Oceanna with a furrow in his brow. "A trap, an unsolvable puzzle. Will they escape? Hear the ticking of the bomb? It creates suspense, damn it! You press the shutter at the moment you see that look. I feel it! Snap it right then. Literally putting my finger on it. Raises the hairs on my neck. It's a nightmare. The train is heading at you. Eminent danger," Dad's eyes bulged as he stared at the dark TV screen.

"Well, umm . . . congratulations . . . Dad." She watched his eyes start to close, drooping repeatedly until they finally fit together after fluttering. He leaned back and drifted off, snoring with his chin on his chest.

The wind ground through the branches outside. The power went out. Oceanna lit candles, hauled in more wood, poured another viscous drink, and let her imagination turn. After an hour of thinking in the dark, she grabbed the phone and called Rose.

6
Having Backs

After sharing Dad's good news with Rose, Oceanna described her experience, hoping it might inspire a story and also offering a chance to vent some frustrations. She encouraged Rose to get the writing instructions out and read the entire article over the phone as she jotted a few notes on how to structure the next great American novel.

"Happy New Year, by the way," Rose said after reading the details to her.

"Let's hope so," Oceanna said. "Okay, here's the summary I have. We need to choose a genre and a theme targeting that audience, summarize the entire novel in one long paragraph, and then go back and create each chapter in one or two paragraphs until the whole plot is developed and done, the characters established, and the major points chosen. That sounds so simple," Oceanna sighed.

"Right, that's going to keep us from wandering off into so many dead ends we can't even follow them or tie them together. The guy says there are no landmarks or paths when you write a book. You have to make the direction from your own head and just develop whatever your style is by yourself," Rose thought about the magnitude of the project. "That's why most people never get a story out, no compass," Rose lit another smoke and coughed. She leaned back in her recliner nest. "So, what is your genre?"

"Lesbian Mystery/Romance. Is that a thing?" Oceanna grinned to herself.

"So, the plot in a mystery story starts with the crime already committed. The murder is done, and you are solving who did it, while in a thriller, the plot is a crime being committed, and the crime is still in motion; that's the difference?" said Rose. "Are you thinking of killing her off in the first chapter?"

"Umm, I don't know. I have to think about this?" Oceanna grunted and tapped her pencil on the yellow pad. She doodled a woman's face on the lower half of the sheet, with several points poking out like horns. Her eyes moved about the room, examining the pictures and memorabilia fitted snugly onto floor-to-ceiling shelves, the full length of the living room, filled with books and vinyl records collected over the family's lifetime. She felt a strong desire to put her own contribution on the shelves, proving that Juanita was not the only kid worth loving. On the other hand, she had long resisted the impulse to compete for approval, refusing to show dependence on the judgment of others. A familiar ugly tug stung her gut. She had to admit she had wanted acknowledgment from her cold and conceited father.

"Why need approval from people who love their vodka more than their children?" she mumbled.

With shame, she admitted to herself that the chaotic relationships with women in search of passion equal to love proved that an early lack of human connection had taken its predictable toll. Oceanna felt humiliated that she had been weak enough to submit to internal forces, making her a statistic. Like it or not, she demonstrated an erratic pattern of broken relationships that placed her on the dysfunction map. She hated to admit it, but she was the quintessential survivor of an alcoholic family.

"Oceanna, are you still there? What are you thinking about?" Rose said.

"I'm realizing this book thing will be a kind of weird journal. I'm being bombarded with past issues. It just struck me; I'm scared?"

She grabbed her tobacco pouch and yanked a paper from the flat of official papers that came with each pouch, pinched a mound of moist shreds between her fingers, dropped them into the folded paper, rolled the cigarette, and stuck it in her mouth. "I've made a lot of mistakes," admitted Oceanna.

"Well, who could blame you? All that craziness and drinking. We all make mistakes. You have to test the path to survive. Everybody has to try out solutions, see what works, and get out. Vulnerabilities, the weak spots," Rose coughed a little, slid a couple of white pills out, and downed them with cold coffee. "I guess writing slows down the memories; it's time to dissect them. In that case, we both have enough material for several books!"

"Ya, some of them comic books," Oceanna smiled.

"Hey, don't put down those graphic novels; I read an article saying that they're on an upturn!" Rose hunted among the piles of magazines on her coffee table, seeking the particular monthly issue, and fingered through the crumpled Detective Mystery magazine, looking for the article.

"My relationships are always with women who want to be taken care of, major drama queens, and I fall for the honeymoon every time the games begin. It's hot at first; things taper off, and I break up. I can't believe I'm going to admit this in a novel?" she rolled her eyes, gulped down the last of her martini, and licked her lips.

Dad snored a soft purr from his chair. Snow let up for a moment, giving way to the bright crescent of a moon that illuminated the snow-covered yard in cobalt blue. A fat owl dropped from her nightly hunt onto a low pine branch near the house. Her weight bounced the bough, shaking loose the snow collected among the needles, creating a cloud of free flakes that blew across the window in front of Oceanna and stared at her through the large window. They focused on each other for minutes. Owl confidently bobbing about on a branch in the wind and snow, woman floundering with the ghosts of the past drunk in a chair. She took it as a sign.

"Listen, friend, let's just know that we control this stuff we are writing, and if we don't want to share it, we don't have to," Rose felt she was being guided and tried to guide Oceanna too. "Let's just explore tragedies and triumphs together. We know I tend to date stalkers!"

Rose shot a glance at the framed picture of her last boyfriend, his skinny face turned down on the shelf, and shuddered. Then, she prayed silently that he would never return. She prayed also that she would have the strength to turn him away if he did show up.

"At least we have the sense enough to have each other as friends, right?" said Rose. "I have your back, and you have mine," she stood up to stretch and get a snack. Her cramps had let up, and she was feeling like she could get some outline started.

"Rose, I'm so glad I'm your friend. You can have my back any time," she felt a twinge of embarrassment, letting her deep affection show. "Oh...you know what I mean."

Rose blushed, too. Being far apart, Rose felt freer to flirt. She had often played flirtation games with Oceanna at parties and clubs, understanding that Oceanna was determined not to date another straight lady. Many stories had Oceanna told about the dangers of lesbians getting caught up in experimental relationship adventures, so Rose figured she could tease with immunity. The pretense was that she was merely playing while in secret, believing that Oceanna possessed all the qualities of an excellent fit.

She admired the look of her mature body, the shine of her smile, the strength of her convictions, the glint in her eye, and their unusual connection. She felt no distance between them, across a table, a room full of people, or thousands of miles across the states.

"So… Are you going to kill her off in the first chapter?" Rose repeated.

Oceanna popped, "Ya, I should love her to death. The End."

They burst into nervous laughter. Oceanna, half drunk, roared and coughed and slopped some of her fresh martini on the yellow writing pad scribbled with several female faces doodled among her outline notes.

Dad opened his eyes once and went back to napping. Rose bent over, chuckling, trying not to strain her belly into more bleeding.

Oceanna gathered her breath, "I'm starting my story like this. Once upon a time… I fell in love with a lady's lap."

Rose cradled the phone under her chin while she fingered the shiny magazine pages, looking for the instructions.

"The most basic elements of capturing the story are outlining the chapters," she whispered, dragging her fingers down the list, reading the steps like the recipe for baking a cake.

"Okay, you have to pick a genre, Lesbian Mystery/Romance, if that is a genre."

"Why? It sounds kind of confining," Oceanna asked.

"It helps you sell the book. The publishers have niches they appeal to, so you have to fit into one of them."

Oceanna stared at her father snoring in his recliner, his thin lips fluttering.

"Mine will involve a bloody murder with several good sex scenes," she smirked.

"I assume not porn?" Rose asked.

"Right, that's my second book."

Rose smiled, "I guess mine is a mystery too, with a female detective that's hard-boiled. I love reading those things, so I think I would love writing it. Maybe based in San Francisco."

"Hey, that's good," Oceanna rolled another smoke, leaned back in her desk chair, listened to Rose flip pages, and watched the smoke roll from her cigarette.

"Okay, let's do the story paragraph," Rose sighed. Her head was hurting, her back ached. She thought about the frustration her story would have to include, disappointed love, and perhaps sloppy revenge. Her thoughts were glued to the day she discovered her boyfriend was married and had an entire family. Blinded by love, she had ignored any sign of cheating. The thought never crossed her mind until his wife called her office phone, begging Rose to shut him out.

The phone was silent for a few moments, and they listened to each other breathe and smoke as they thought about their stories.

"Rose, I'm seeing this stuff as if it were a nightmare journal, in a way. The situations were bad enough the first time," Oceanna puffed.

"Well, now we can redirect. I don't have to stop in the same places. We can reinvent," said Rose, envisioning herself being trapped in Ken's office, squirming under the pressure while praying to avoid humiliation. She winced, jerking her coffee, sloshing brown over the rim onto her sleeve.

Oceanna recalled the embarrassment of discovering she had been replaced by another woman but still could not stop missing the beautiful smoothness of her lover's breasts and the sweetness of her taste. Falling in love had been easy. Why couldn't the honeymoon last?

"This is going to be some kind of adventure, that's for sure," she mumbled.

7

Intrusion

---

ang! Bang! Clang, whirr! Snap, snap. Head confined in a plastic harness and under firm instructions not to move, she breathed anxiously. Drained from emotional stress and loss of blood, Rose's mind drifted into fantasy, dreaming beyond the magnets and X-ray beams that spied into her flesh, hunting for the enemy.

The gigantic medical marvel turned and spun, focusing its robotic eyes on her living parts, taking pictures of every inch of organ, bone, and muscle. Every lump and freckle radiated, viewed incrementally. Technicians looked for dark spots that could be telling. Every suspicious density was targeted. Any abnormality that crowded her healthy meat, any suspicious mass, was going to be rooted out and biopsied. The experts looked with inescapable microscopes for hives of disease. The ugly spots. She worried about the thing making her bleed, confining her to her recliner, leaving her wasted. She feared she would not escape becoming a hemorrhaging shut-in at the age of thirty-five, and then the beast would kill her.

Uncomfortable and purposefully over-medicated, Rose started to numb. She felt the bones of her hips and elbows anchoring against the smooth surfaces and relaxing against the examination tube in which she was confined. A necessary evil is the tightness of the electronic eye's table. She itched in the spots where her absorbent pads stuck to her skin, another necessary evil, preventing an embarrassing mess on the equipment. With the fear of shaming herself in mind, Rose drifted off into a daydream. The test noises faded. The clamber of the MRI mechanisms meshed with her dream, evolving into the sound of blowing truck horns and the roar of tow motors, ringing of phones echoing through the A.A.S. warehouse, reverberating off the high metal roof like an old familiar song, longed for and refreshing.

Rose dreamed her feet clicked along the acres of white cement floor, along isles of heavy metal shelves, fifty feet high, stacked with parts and pieces of hundreds of packaging projects waiting for the nimble and not-so-nimble fingers of the workers. Assembly line tables were arranged strategically with materials, stretched a hundred feet down the center of the long open space, with assembly stations set in at intervals and arranged for the accommodation of each worker's needs—organization for efficiency and productivity at the daily grind.

Jobs that may seem tedious and repetitive to some were welcomed at A.A.S. by workers, grinning as they stomped and rolled in from the beeping busses each morning. Ready workers found their stations, hung their hats, secreted their lunch boxes under their seats, waved hello at each other, and hugged the supervisors. Some folks came in angry, frustrated by complicated people's problems, and needed someone to listen to them, a friend they could trust, like Rose.

Having grown up in a religious family dedicated to doing their piece of the lord's work by adopting disabled children, Rose was patient. Her Parents bravely endured the rigors of rescuing children, considered broken, from antiquated asylums intended to treat them that became prisons.

Removing fragile children from overcrowded nurseries was overdue. Children restrained in cribs for weeks, forgotten, rarely touched, neglected, and abused, had become necessary after the horrors of life in "Asylums for the feeble-minded" had been exposed in the '70s.

Hundreds of children became adults while they lived their entire lives behind it's locked gates, never knowing anything else. Finally, after years of operation and many suspicious deaths, outraged families brought heavy lawsuits for abuse, bringing the institutions down for good. While growing up, Rose had accepted their uniqueness, being told by her mother that the kids were brothers and sisters, teaching her to love them as whole people.

Anxiety tingled up her spine. A chill ran through her. Sweat beaded up on her brow as she felt her mood shift to the dark side. Her dream took a sour turn. She found her face flattened against Ken Musk's office door, leaving her pink face powder on a brass name plate, reading "FROGGY," the tip of her nose flat, nudging into the capital letters.

He yelled for her to enter. It was an order. The door swung open smoothly, sucking her into the dimly lit room, levitating her paralyzed body to the edge of his oversized black desk. Her bare feet dangling an inch off the floor, stiff and still. She became entangled in strands of transparent plastic shrink wrap. Snaking into the room, it uncoiled itself from the packaging machine and knotted around her ankles, trapping her. The glow of Ken's computer screen illuminated his jowls. His bulging eyes glide in their sockets, tracking movement like a cat tracking mice. His masculine scent overwhelmed the air in the room, gaging her.

Ken drew his sweaty thumbs deep into his flabby thighs to dry them and to hint at his intentions. Standing up, he unbuckled his belt and came around the desk. His eyes roamed over Rose's full chest heaving with her gasps. She was his captured prey, ready for his consumption. She wept and hugged her knees close in an attempt to get out, twisting but remaining stuck.

She considered the price of compromising, letting him win with no struggle, taking the path of several other women in the shop. He might reward her. Could she live with becoming a contributor to the arrogance she hated? Should she lose her awkward integrity in exchange for remaining to fight another day? Toying with using subterfuge instead, she considered taking the risk of becoming a crawling agent of change by inviting the devil into a tender trap.

"What could possibly go wrong?" she moaned.

She felt the conceit of his stiff body pull up against her from the rear. His hands traced her hips, grabbing at her breasts as though they were his. The computer screen light cast their chaotic shadows on the walls as she slapped at his lewd fingers. Her nostrils stung with the thick smell of his whisky breath. She shuddered at the abrasion of coarse bristles on her neck while he chewed on her.

Timidly, the office doorknob rattled. Rose thought she had detected the door clicking and prayed desperately for someone to help her. Tammy, Ken's loyal executive secretary, tip-toed in on sharp, high heels, carrying a pile of folders for Ken to sign, unsurprised by the unfolding rape in front of her. She had seen it many times before. She ran her free hand down Ken's wet back as she plopped the folders down, showing no concern. Rose screamed for help, straining her lungs, and to her astonishment, a fourth shadow appeared on the wall.

A child-sized man appeared in the door frame, and then Vernon stomped into the room. Rose's favorite client came to the rescue. Standing firmly in the doorway, four-foot, ten-inch-tall, a moral man with a sunken chest, thinning hair, and flexing arms soft and slack rope had come to her aide.

Vernon was squinty-eyed and scrawny but had arrived with heroic intentions. Fists jammed on his narrow hips, his pants sagging, synched past the very last holes in his belt, giving him the appearance of a tote bag full of bones. His head was so small, and his hair so thin. He seemed like a baby more than a man. He grinned a wide, rubbery grin, commanding Ken to stop in language that he made up all by himself. It was his spirit that commanded respect, not his vocabulary.

An unlikely hero, born unable to reproduce language, he growled and grunted at the spectacle before him. Damsels in distress provoked him into risky chivalry. He arched his crooked spine to stick out his chest, tore open his vest, and gestured for Ken to notice the picture on his T-shirt of his favorite television wrestler, depicted in vibrant colors, standing over his defeated foe, grimacing.

Vern pointed at his own face, delivering a similar twisted expression, warning him he meant business while his tiny teeth gnashed. Vernon was uniquely wise. He had developed a flamboyant pantomime language of his own. He made animal sounds and gestured at Ken to stop or else stomped his little feet and panted hard.

"Really Vernon? You're a fake, strong man, buddy! Only a big man in your small head." Ken taunted. "Ya! Boo-hoo, dummy. You want to see a real man at work? Watch this!" He smiled as he tugged Rose's dress, ripping it off.

Rose screamed. Her hands were so wet with sweat that she lost her grip on the desk. Vernon strode up to Ken's exposed rear end, paced off the distance he needed, precisely, saluted, and swung back his foot to get momentum. Gathering all his might, he drove a direct kick between Ken's twitching legs, dropping him, shocked, to the floor.

"Just like on the wrestling channel," peeped Ken.

The shrink wrap around Rose's legs came loose and crawled around Ken, who lay in a heap, slithering about his arms and torso, crackling as it turned under his helpless carcass, creeping around his hips and neck.

Rose rolled up onto the desk, gasping, covering her open dress with manila folders. Vernon stood coolly over Ken, dusting his hand off with a couple of short claps. Slowly, reaching into his overstuffed pants pockets and pulling out a fat cigar, he mimed a request for a light from Tammy. Withdrawing a giant, red-tipped stick match from her cleavage, she struck it on Ken's bald spot. He snatched the match from her fingers, lit his smoke that billowed with each puff, and touched Ken with the fire end. Plastic bonds ignited, bursting him into flame. He did not move, accepting his fate in silence.

Vernon tiptoed up to Rose and offered his midget hand to help her down. Rose admired Vernon from the first. His bravery emanated from the confidence in his heart.

"Ma'am, wake up. You're moving," latex-covered hands touched her shoulders, shaking her slightly up to a thick wakefulness. Rose peeped out, returning, groggy, to the reality of the narrow MRI table. Her dream lingered in her head as she apologized and promised to stay still this time. The nurse checked her alignments and sent her back under, fingers crossed.

She allowed herself the guilty pleasure of feeling satisfaction watching Vernon kill the beast, envisioning Ken's ridiculous expression as Vernon popped him one of his favorites. She thought about her book and began to organize the characters into a possible plot. If it didn't sell, at least she could vicariously rein victorious. Miraculously, it made her feel better, even while stuck in the tube.

After the medical imaging was finished, she pulled on her clothes, padding her underwear with an extra-large absorbent pad for the long bus ride home. She walked gingerly through the glistening hospital halls and hesitated at the vista windows overlooking the misty

Willamette Valley, with an unencumbered line of sight over 50 miles, all the way to the white peak of Mt. Hood. Portland city lights were coming on, twinkling at Rose.

Pulling tight the collar of her coat, she loaded onto the bus for the winding road back home. She unfolded a bus schedule from her pocket and scribbled plot ideas in the margins, taking her eyes off the paper long enough to gaze at the romantic view of the Emerald City as the wheels trundled along, missing Oceanna all the way.

8

Snow blind

Three feet of snow piled high in the ditches on either side of the main road, now an ice sheet, as the faint orange sun set on Montville. Dad's sturdy, tricked-out Jeep trundled confidently down Route 528 at forty miles per hour, all four wheels propelling Oceanna and her dozing father over hollers and hills, blanketed in ice and snow, on their way to the last client named on a long list of shut-ins that had been issued to Oceanna by the Department of Disabilities.

The stock market crash of 2008 had shattered both of their investments – savings invested and pensions – forcing Oceanna to return to social work, serving disabled people fortunate enough to be still able to live in their private homes by dropping by each week and performing wellness checks.

She was given an address list of homes on rural farms needing ongoing support. She made personal contact with isolated farmers needing weekly checks for daily basics such as medical problems, food and meal preparation, and possibly requesting delivered lunches or housekeeping assistance while developing a trusting relationship, which is considered paramount.

She insisted that Dad come along for his own safety. Wobbling around on his weak legs often posed a risk for falling, and because he had a working understanding of off-road directions. Dad had intimate knowledge of the gravel roads running along the boundaries between Amish farms. The narrow gravel buggy paths that ran along the farmers' network of abutting properties provided safer paths for horse traffic, frequently including buggies, the cozy back boxes on wheels, stuffed with families, tightly squeezed in, traveling to gatherings, weddings, and funerals, and home churches, pulled by lanky horses, trotting purposefully, unflappable and graceful.

The gas engine tractors hauling mountains of corn and hay could lumber for miles at slow paces without blocking faster vehicles. Enormous farming machines festooned with complicated wheels and pulleys with long metal arms fitted with sharp discs for plowing could move from field to field in safety. Harvest wagons filled high to overflowing, lugged by teams of muscular brown Shire horses, moved between farms, sharing manpower and supplies.

The hidden network of miles of private paths assured farmers they could roll at their own paces, getting to the fields and friends as needed, freeing the semi-trucks and commuters to careen down the asphalt at their own risks.

Dad told hair-raising stories about racing through the uncharted paths, arriving at house and barn fires ahead of the water tankers and volunteer firefighters after catching the first alerts on his stacked array of police and sheriff trackers and emergency responder radio sets bolted between the front seats of the Jeep.

Black boxes tucked into every available bit of leg room that could be spared blinked red lights and squawked when action was in progress, links to the wild world, vital to newsmen and no less than spiritual to this retired ambulance chaser.

Jack Pontiac was known for careening to disasters in a tricked-out rig, oversized tires scattering gravel and dust, hood rigged with a flashing red emergency strobe light, with a mad gleam in his pale blue eyes and a sly grin across his square jaw.

The stories volunteer fire fighters told about him brought smiles to his face as he relived the fun of being bounced around over the countryside, covering local tragedies, risking life and limb to get there, then giving his pictures to the Good News Gazette for free. He laughed to see his Hollywood-perfect photos of burning barns squeezed between the grocery store sales coupons and listings for sales of piglets, milk cows, and dog breeders. It made him a local curiosity, familiar to virtually everyone in the community.

The plows had been out this freezing evening. Roaring diesel trucks fitted with flashing green and yellow warning lights and heavy metal scoops buckled to their front bumpers shaved the surface of the road to ice-rink smooth. Flinging snow to the side, hurling rocks and ice into yards and windshields as they sped past, presenting necessary hazards.

Off-road snow clearing was done by hand with shovels and pickup trucks with scoops at a slower pace, carefully manicuring the long driveways and inroads to the farmhouses and barns and over the buggy paths.

Oceanna turned here and there under her father's direction, winding their way to the next location. Inquisitive Amish children peeped out the back doors of the narrow carriages, huddled together against the cold. They stared at the Jeep, giggling and waving secretly with fresh smiles. Traditionally dressed in thick black, handmade coats with required bonnets on each little girl and black knit caps on every boy. They gawked at the Jeep as Oceanna passed them on the left when the path was wide enough to allow it. Dad waved thanks at whoever held the reins, usually a ruddy-faced man with the traditional long, untrimmed beard, who bobbed his head in a somber return. The horse's breath billowing out of flared nostrils, never reacted, holding a steady pace, trotting, eyes straight ahead.

Dad and Oceanna rolled along in matching red plaid coats, fleece lined. Father sported the plaid coveralls to match and fleece-lined boots. Overdressed was better than underdressed when it came to Dad. He seemed to live in perpetual chill, his aging skin thinning, letting the heat out. He was wrapped like a Christmas present sans the bow.

The Jeep engine and transmission had been fully rebuilt after a remarkable four hundred thousand miles, revitalizing the heater, which blasted the passengers with super-hot air at the knees, sweating Oceanna but pleasing Dad.

Dense fog encapsulated the lowlands, creating pools of complete invisibility. Ghostly shadows of farmhouses in shades of silver and lighter and darker grays seemed to float in the distance. Vague human shapes appeared and disappeared in currents of mist, like spirits of long-gone pioneers haunting. Trees gathered in slate-colored forests, only the lower trunks and limbs visible. The crowns were so high and the mist so dense that the tops of old oaks and maples disappeared.

Light snow fell, not sticking to the windshield but blowing away like confetti, obscuring visibility, irritating Oceanna as she searched for numbers painted on fences or nailed to trees or landmarks Dad described to her.

"Loves Farm . . . Dad, that's the last stop, do you know it? I mean, have you been there?" said Oceanna, squinting at the fog.

Oceanna read the name off the profile page of the county's file on the last client, Gretchen Loves. She checked the GPS suction-cupped to the windshield, but the buggy paths did not show up. GPS thought she was in the middle of a field and kept asking to recalculate. She muted the mechanical voice in frustration.

Dad shook his head and continued to look out the window.

"No, I've never been there, but I passed it now and then, I think," he pointed at a tall, dark barn shape to the right. "I think that's John Burkholder's place. His family moved here 200 years ago. That barn is over a hundred years old," he pointed out the frosty window. "I remember stories of a tragedy at Love's farm," he scratched his face and smeared the condensation on the passenger window with his glove, trying to clear a peephole.

"They were horse trainers?" asked Oceanna.

"Ya. Have you seen the buggy trainers going along the road? The light training rigs. It's just a chariot without the frills, I guess, running up and down 528. They have to start on dirt tracks before they get to that point." Dad said.

The road descended steeply until the mist became a charcoal gel into which the Jeep submerged. The row of extra fog lights on the bumper could not penetrate the fog. They seemed to butt up against a solid. The ice-white surface of the path and the dim headlight blended together completely, obscuring any boundaries or roadside markers.

"We could be on the edge of a cliff or upside down for all I can see! Crap!" Oceanna slowed to a crawl, fearing she would drive them into a ditch.

She opened her door, stuck her head out, and bent her face down as close to the road as she could to locate the edge of the road by following the scrape mark the scoop made along as they plowed snowbanks. At least she knew they were on the road, kept it moving, and hoped to drive out of the murk eventually.

"Minus twenty degrees by the dash thermometer, Dad. Are you all right with the door open?" She glanced at Dad, who grinned and rubbed his hands together in short, rapid movements, holding his fingers close to the blasting heat vents aimed at his knees.

"I'm having a great time, dear. This is my kind of thing!" He faked a maniacal cackle.

"Super! Dad, do you have any idea where the hell we are?" she continued to creep along, leaning out the door, one hand on the steering wheel, one foot leaning on the running board, the other hand clinging to the door, swinging out, straining to keep an eye on the edge and avoid falling over.

"Well… have we gone about 1-mile past Burkholder's?" he asked.

She glanced rapidly at the speedometer, "Ya, about that."

"Are we going west or southwest?" He pictured the landscape in his mind. He recalled several bends in the road and the low spot like the one they had found themselves in now. He recalled a shabby wooden bridge over a creek in a deep gully Amish boys fished from in summer.

Oceanna glanced at the direction on the GPS screen. "Yep, the monitor says we are in the middle of a field, going west, near the Cuyahoga River." She slammed on the brakes and slid to a halt.

The dark uprights of a split-rail fence appeared on the left edge of the path. The posts were giving way with age, leaning randomly after years of heavy snow. Following it for a hundred feet, there stood a pair of crumbling river stone pillars. Eight feet tall, thick around and out of plum. Tipping slightly but intact. They indicated an entry to a larger estate. Gate markers were often used to demarcate the entrance to the original farms before the Civil War.

This antique entrance with crumbling mortar falling out from between the round brown and gray stones, elegantly topped with wooden carvings of rearing horses, was an inroad to a groomed driveway leading to a house.

Oceanna guessed they had reached the rear entrance of somebody's farm. If they could make it to the main house, a house still standing and occupied, they could ask for directions to Loves, or at least they could orient themselves and get back on Route 528. She shut the driver's door decisively and looked mournfully at Dad.

"Well, it is a plowed driveway?" she sighed. "It could be worse."

Dad straightened his glasses and smiled, "If we are lucky, it will."

"You're kind of spooky, Dad," she mumbled and turned slowly onto the path.

The lane was narrow, inclined at a gradual angle, and had been carefully plowed, but it seemed forbidding. The moment the taillights crossed the pillars, she felt a sadness envelop her. As they crept along, the melancholy intensified, sucking the optimism out of her. Oceanna tried to shrug it off, identifying her anxiety as a simple reaction to the thick fog and the loss of a certain direction.

"This used to be nice, I bet," she said as they followed the crooked split rails and leafless trees. Her scalp prickled, raising short hairs on her neck.

Dad was quiet, straining to see some markers. His body bobbed and rocked as they trundled over the divots at a snail's pace. The field gave way to a dense orchard of gnarled fruit trees. Several large branches had sheared off and lay scattered across the path, blocking the way. She shifted into the park, left the rig idling, and climbed out to drag them off. She became aware of a lack of any sounds of life. No birds chirping, no cow or dog calling, and even the engine purr was dampened—a desolate zone. Complete stillness surrounded them. She hurried back into the driver's seat.

"It's too late to go back, so here we go," she shuddered and continued to crawl forward at a mile and hour.

Finally, a row of ancient apple trees lined the path. Withered fruit dangled, black and scrawny from fragile limbs, and then a low stone wall of the same river rocks as the pillars appeared from under the plowed mounds of snow. Finally, there appeared lights. Square yellow lights could be seen through the mist. Civilization at last and something living.

Climbing the widening drive, the fog thinned, revealing the frame of a two-story house built of massive logs with a cobble stone walk and steps that wound up to a wide porch, leading to a solid hand-crafted door with a rearing horse carved into the center panel.

Yellow light flickered in the lower-story windows. Logs weighing thousands of pounds had been lifted and fitted tight, stacked one on the other, creating an imposing, rugged structure with oversized square apertures for windows sunk deep into the logs. The enormous rock chimney dominated one side of the house, billowing smoke.

Cautiously, Oceanna pulled up to the stone steps, letting the Jeep idle while she and Dad stared at the glimmering yellow windows dotting the weighty structure, gauging how much effort it was going to take to assist Dad to reach the front door. Then the front door opened, and a single shape of a short, stout human looked back at them, rocking back and forth, trading weight from one tip toe to the other, waving festively at them to come, like the passengers waving hello at the return of a cruise ship.

Oceanna couldn't be certain if the creature was male or female. It had features of both: a wide torso fitted with broad rolling shoulders and thick, muscled arms fitted with chunky hands that flapped like flags. She could not testify to it being old or young, but it was agile. The barrel-shaped torso was reminiscent of a pillowy matron. The stout pony-like legs ended in dainty feet.

The unsettling combination of parts recalled a spoiled toddler reaching for cookies on a high shelf. The mesmerizing shape disappeared into the house, leaving the door wide open. A broad stone fireplace and mantel twinkled as it reflected the radiant fire below.

"Well… dear?" Dad said, "An adventure is upon us."

They glanced at each other, back at the glowing entrance, and back at each other again.

The canes Dad used in winter had been fitted with short, gripping spikes on the tips for traction. Oceanna pulled them from behind his seat, turned off the engine, and opened the passenger door.

On the count of one, two, three, Oceanna spun his knees in a smooth sweep, stuck the canes in his trembling hands, and lowered him to the ground. His black boots, also tread-enhanced, held him to the slick drive. Snow began to fall more steadily, elevating Oceanna's anxiety to high.

"God forbid we should get stuck here!" she mumbled.

9
Over the thresh hold.

Together, they landed one foot in front of the other, crushing the new snow under the heel, until they stood at the door, looking in.

"I have to use the bathroom," Dad announced. He elbowed his way free of his human tether and stepped over the threshold into the long open living space, sticking his canes into the rough wooden floor, aiming down the hall for a door that might lead to a lavatory.

Oceanna's trepidation gave way to her curiosity as her eyes cast over the framed oil paintings of horses wearing blue ribbons, bookshelves, and a vinyl record collection with hundreds of albums lining the dark log walls. Hundreds of handmade rag dolls lined the top of the shelves, each with a distinct expression and button eyes that seemed to follow her around the room as she snuck by. The leather furniture was old but well-tended. The fireplace was stacked with wood, burning eagerly, lighting the room in a fluttering golden glow. The air smelled of lamp oil and cookies.

"Hello? I'm with the county? We wonder if we could use the bathroom," Oceanna called out.

Praying the resident was not fetching a gun. She yelled, "We live down the road, and we got lost and need a little help. We were looking for Gretchen Love's farm."

Gretchen halted in front of her bedroom mirror when she heard her name called out. Standing barefoot on her fir rug, her calloused toes curled into the dense wolf fur, soothing her anxiety.

She didn't think she was in trouble again. The sheriff hadn't been to her house in years. Living alone freed her from having to apologize or feel awkward or unwelcome. She longed for friends and wrestled with the shame that she did not fit in anywhere. It was easier to pop in and out of places, like when she sold her eggs to the Mullet's Cafe or took her dolls to the big flea market in Middlefield, or when she shopped through the outdoor farmer's bazaar and market.

She always had her coveralls and cowboy hat on in those places. Mostly, she looked like a man on purpose, inserting herself safely into the community, wearing her father's leather coat and boots. Gretchen figured disguising her femininity got her respect—that and the 45-caliber pistol she holstered.

"Safer with it than without it," Father said many times. So, it never left her side. It simplified things. Experience had taught her that females had to be ready to act like killers, too.

She pulled on her coveralls, arranged her gun, tucked in her flannel shirt, and buckled the straps. Eyeing the collection of her fabric dolls set around the room, she listened for which one was right to take along. Which friend would hold her steady, whispering to her with good advice? Who could keep her secrets?

Each figure had seemed to whisper to her, appearing to her as dusty clouds, spiraling smoke, or grey mice, asking to be crafted just so. Each choice in design, fabric, texture, and color had been a request made by the spirit that needed a place to inhabit. Spirits whispered patterns she was to follow for sewing the right kind of bodies they would occupy, making them solid vessels of magic, inspired and ready to assist her.

After years of isolation, she had crafted a warm collection of rag companions, surrounding herself with "family." Animal shapes with animal traits often became intertwined with human bodies, limbs, and faces. Some friends were strong and aggressive. Some friends were sensitive and discrete. But every friend lived.

The most trusted doll, Maxine, with her narrow cheeks and long nose, called to her that she was the one. Her upright cat ears may be useful for listening for dangerous conversations, she suggested. Stuffing the small doll into her breast pocket, she felt confident. She pounded her bare heels down the attic's spiral staircase on the third floor, along the hall between the second-level rooms, and down the wide polished wood staircase to the bathroom.

Footsteps could be heard upstairs, roaming around. Oceanna hoped the owner understood the situation and was prepared to greet them. Dad found the bathroom with an antique-style flushing toilet, got assistance undoing his coveralls, and sat on the throne just in time.

After several minutes, a heavy fist knocked, rattling the bathroom door and scaring Oceanna. Dad flinched, causing him to abruptly kick his feet out in front of him as he sat, clobbering Oceanna hard in the shin.

Oceanna screamed and bent over to hold her bruised shin while she reached for the doorknob. The door blasted open, hitting her on the top of her skull. Her knitted cap softened the blow.

"Morning," Gretchen announced with an anxious smile. Pretending to be undisturbed by the strangers in her home. She stuck out a thick hand in greeting. Oceanna shook her hand, feeling the solid strength running through it.

Gretchen grinned nervously, showing a fence of straight teeth, too small for an adult mouth, dotting thick red gums like white sprinkles on a pink cake. Her plump cheeks, covered with freckles on her puffy face, were as round as a melon, shiny and pale. Her baby-like features were contrasted by the full dark shadow of stubble over her jaw and chin. The smell of aftershave lingered on her fresh shave. Her tall forehead and receding hairline emphasized her thick, reddish eyebrows that lifted and fell cartoonishly.

"Oh, sorry for just coming in?" Oceanna fumbled. "I am the home health worker for the county. I am looking for Gretchen. Is that you?"

Gretchen's eyes fluttered rapidly; her hands clapped together several times. "I knew someone was going to come. I got a letter," she pinched her large round eyes together. "I can't read the letters, but I looked at mark, so I thought maybe a person would come. The lady at Mullet's reads my letters for me. They help me!" she giggled.

"You mean Mary Mullet's Cafe on 528? Ya, we eat there too," Oceanna patted her stomach.

"Hey! Get me out of here. I'm done!" Dad grumbled, feeling exposed and abandoned. He raised a cane and tapped the door.

"Oh, Ya. Gretchen, I had to bring my father today; I take care of him and…"

Gretchen pushed the bathroom door fully open with a swift, confident sweep of her arms, exposing Dad seated on the throne, red plaid coveralls around his ankles, struggling to lift off.

"That's ok. Father's ok. Use the bathroom. Be cozy!" In a sing-song voice, she repeated herself several times and walked purposefully down the long hall to the living room.

After Dad was put back together, they stepped into the blazing fireplace in the living room. He got stationed in a large leather recliner next to the fireplace and seemed to be drifting off to sleep. Gretchen perked coffee in a large coffee-stained percolator on a shelf built into the hearth. The glass bulb on the lid showed the popping coffee brewing with a slurping sound as it hissed. Gretchen watched the color of the coffee change from light brown to almost black in the bulb.

"Black but not Burnt!" she reported firmly.

She fitted a worn hot mitt over her hand and poured three ceramic mugs of steaming coffee. From a cold silver pitcher, she poured thick cream and dumped three spoons full of sugar into each, stirred with a short wooden spoon, and handed the cups to her guests. Dad had to set his on the side table next to him, sloshing on to his white undershirt shirt.

The nervous hostess got him a short dish towel for his bib. Leaning over him, she pressed the grip of her .45 caliber into his arm.

"Do you always wear a gun?" Dad questioned while admiring the quality of her weapon.

Gretchen smiled and patted her holster. "It's a cowboy Colt .45. I used to think it was heavy, but now I have the balance. I never take it off. That's my code."

"What's the carving on the leather?" he asked, reaching out and leaning forward to get a closer look.

She put her hip out, leaned on the chair arm near Dad's elbow, and bragged. "It's a real Mexican leather holster, carved with a girl riding a bronco! You don't see that a lot," she said proudly.

She traced the edges of the figure with her finger. "See? That is a girl rider, and that is a big Mexican hat called a sombrero," she patted the holster.

"Is that a handmade rosewood grip?" he twittered while eyeing the pink wood, crafted with shallow groves to match a left-handed personal grip.

"Yep! I'm a lefty, so I had to have a special grip. My father made that for me," she sighed and went back to the couch next to Oceanna.

Dad stared at her, amazed. "I have a gun with a teak grip I made for myself... because I am left-handed," he smiled at her, and she smiled back nervously. She felt the doll turn around in her pocket as a warning not to share too much.

Oceanna got out the file, opened it, and started to assess Gretchen.

"It seems like you are doing really well taking care of yourself. The file says you live here alone. No guardian, just the bank trustee, and Social Security, right?"

Oceanna hoped to get the business done before the snow piled up on the roads. Except for the snowflakes falling near the windows, nothing could be seen, especially on the back roads that had no streetlights. The night was so dark you would not see your hand in front of your face. If the snow and the night fell on you, it was possible to get stuck until sunup.

"Right!" she grinned enthusiastically, slurping coffee between answers.

"You have a payee that manages the money? The bank in Middlefield manages the trust your father left you," she looked up to read her facial expression.

"Yes, ma'am!" Gretchen looked back at Oceanna. "I do it all myself. I take care of my chickens in the barn, pick up eggs, and sell 'em. I sew my dolls. Some want to go to the farmer's market."

"How do you get there?" Dad chimed in. "It's eight miles to town."

"I drive my four-wheel bike. My father taught me!" she used a thick handheld about thigh level to demonstrate her height at the time. "I plow my road. I have a big green tractor," she flinched.

A grotesque facial tick took over the corners of her mouth, drawing her cheeks back in a tight grimace. She rubbed her face hard with her palm, relaxing it after a moment. Oceanna was quiet and observant.

"What happened to your family?" Dad asked directly.

"I'll ask the questions, Dad, if you don't mind," Oceanna glanced over at him, spilling coffee on his bib.

"I have pictures!" Gretchen popped up off the couch with a jolt, moving directly to a stack of newspapers yellowing among the books and records. She tenderly picked up a moldering twenty-year-old edition of the *Montvillian Newsletter*, delivering it to Oceanna's lap with a plop. A cloud of dust floated up from the front-page photo.

"Read it to me, please! That's me, that's my dad, and that is his horse!" she announced while scratching her freshly shaved cheeks, then plopped down on the couch closer to Oceanna. She pointed at the photo of a short man who looked just like her, with the same plump cheeks, high forehead, and heavy shadow of a beard on his chin. He wore a straw hat and coveralls, proudly holding the reins of a magnificent palomino stallion, with a large blue first-place ribbon hanging from its bridle, named *Lake Pearl*, looking into the flash.

Standing next to him was a chubby, twelve-year-old girl in matching coveralls. Her round face exhibited a bitter frown, scowling at the camera. The headline read, "Slaughter at Loves Farm," in giant type.

Oceanna inhaled deeply, taking a moment to collect herself, strategizing how to react to a story about the slaughter of Gretchen's father, Gustoff Loves, and his prize horse, *Lake Pearl*. Gretchen rocked side to side in her seat with a grin on her face, seemingly oblivious to the tragic quality of the story in the paper.

Quickly scanning the article, Oceanna smiled and said, "Wow, Dad, this is quite a picture. Look and tell us what you think."

She stood up and took several steps to hang the paper close to his face. Her back turned to Gretchen, who was waiting eagerly to hear the story. Dad looked at the large type, his eyes moving over the photo, then up at Oceanna, showing a distressed expression.

"Oh! Ya, Gretchen… this is a loo- loo!" He spoke in an uncharacteristically kind and almost sensitive voice.

"Something is wrong!" Gretchen felt the little doll in her pocket wiggle her velvet cat ears in the direction of Dad's questions. Gretchen became still and listened. Her doll whispered, "She thinks you did something bad."

Oceanna returned to the couch. Sitting next to Gretchen, she felt the atmosphere chill in a matter of moments. Looking into her client's face, she became fixated. Transforming in front of her eyes, Gretchen's giddy persona gave way, exposing her emotions through a painful change in her expression. The deeply guarded agony boiled up like roiling bubbles convulsing from the bottom of a lake. Gretchen transformed into an entirely different person, from humble and open to hard and defensive.

One moment, she seemed to believe there was a happy story about her father and herself winning a prize, showing no sign of remorse or anxiety. The next moment reflects paranoia.

Oceanna pondered how she could be unaware of her father being slaughtered in the barn, along with his stallion, as the article described. Could Gretchen have been so traumatized that she blacked out the memory? Where was her mother in all this? Did her mother kill Gustoff and go to prison, or what? She thought. Oceanna smiled stiffly at Gretchen.

"This is a story about you and your father and a beautiful horse named Lake Pearl," she pointed to the first line of the article.

"Right! That's right," Gretchen said flatly through clinched teeth.

"It says something bad happened to your father one day. It's an accident or something. Is that right? Did something happen in the barn?" Oceanna braced herself for a reaction.

"I don't know what happened!" Cheek muscles undulated along her wide jaw.

She stared at the image under Oceanna's fingertip on the newspaper lying across her lap. She felt the ugly hardening start in her chest again. It hadn't taken over for a long time. She hated the feeling of going hard and sad and far. Her feet felt flat. Her insides become as solid as cement. She hated the hardening that came on when people were mean. Her teeth clinched; a jolt of pain radiated through her molars. Images started to return to her. She shook her head and clamped her eyes shut, trying to stop her memories. She covered her eyes with her palms, grinding her face into her hands.

Oceanna sat as still as possible, uncertain of how to gather the situation up and secure a working relationship. She thought she should comfort Gretchen but was not sure how.

Her thoughts rolled, "What the hell happened? What was Gretchen's part in this thing?" she wondered as her fragile client disintegrated before her.

Gretchen stood robotically, silently, and walked upstairs. Her bare feet pounded along the ceiling above Dad and Oceanna as they sat in silence, clutching the coffee mugs, muffling as she got further away until the sound of a door sliding shut finished the retreat into silence.

10
Like a Dream

"**S**o, here it is, Rose!" said Oceanna, wondering about the cause of the background clatter on Rose's end of the line. Inspired by at least one plot idea she'd had to develop suspense, Oceanna continued to blurt rough ideas for some tension-building elements she could include in her story.

"It starts with the death of Yvonne Ford's deceitful lover, Candice Jamm. The gorgeous Candice incinerates into ashes in an apartment fire, suspiciously set by an unknown arson. Yvonne becomes the most obvious suspect because everyone knows Candice sleeps around with other women, like all her friend's partners, making many jealous enemies, right? But Yvonne is the closest and probably the most humiliated, so she is the first suspect. Plus, Candice and Yvonne fought in the strip bar where Candice danced the night before during her twenty-first birthday party! They all got drunk and had an old-fashioned bar room brawl with the cake thrown all over, half-dressed dancers scattering into the parking lot and everything! Later, there is a passionate make-up love scene, including parts of the birthday cake and candles! What do you think of that as an opener?"

Praying, terrified, and shaking, hearing Oceanna's voice but not the meaning of her words, Rose held the phone to her ear and put one foot in front of the other, robotically, down the polished hall of the new wing in the University Hospital on Portland's rocky west hills and up the elevator to the fifth floor, oncology.

Riding up the glass elevator, she could not appreciate the breathtaking view of the glaciated volcanic cone, fifty miles across the lush pine forests of the Willamette Valley or feel tempted to a steaming hot brew of fancy from the coffee cart in the hall. Her feet clunked along on the ends of her reluctant legs, feeling as brittle and lifeless as plaster. She knew she was moving, directing her course through the gauntlet of medical reception areas and exam rooms, but her mind could not come along. She had to block it.

The thought of a long, slow decline, so often experienced with cancer, horrified her. She had witnessed the effects of cancer on a body when she took care of her mother, who died of it. The smell of... death. She began to weep silently. Tears trickled down her cold cheeks. Her nose dripped. She pulled out a tissue and wiped it, stuffing the tissue back in her pocket with trembling fingers.

The thought of collapsing and dropping dead in the hall brought a level of peace. Getting it over with quickly may be all she could hope for.

"I'm taking you in with me, Anna… Just stay on the line… please," she said.

She hit the silver button for wheelchair access, and the glass doors glided open silently. The reception nurse was young, polite, and dressed in scrubs with a pattern of lively children playing, instructing Rose to sit. Her trained eye assessed the level of shock Rose was going through.

"Sit down, honey… before you fall down," the nurse said to herself.

Gripping the phone, clinging to the line, her best friend cried too. The thought of losing Rose, not having her in her life, intruded as a real possibility for the first time. Aloneness burned into her heart, triggering panic. Oceanna closed her eyes and imagined herself holding Rose tight to her chest, becoming an emotional sponge, absorbing the hurt and fear. She found herself weeping at the detached sound in Rose's voice.

Rose spoke in short comments when responding to doctors, restraining a scream and outrage. The measured kind of voice that agrees and complies with orders. Answers are given when forced to communicate politely, with the understanding that she must give others control, or else, but backed by resolve and dignity, retaining the right to say no, even if it comes out shaky.

Oceanna closed her eyes, her hand held over her mouth to muffle whimpers whistling out. She was desperate for good news but braced for dreadful possibilities and gripped with the desire to go through every second with her beloved friend. The roller coaster was theirs together.

She couldn't hold her body close even if she were in the same room. That had been the relationship's operating rule since the beginning, set to avoid damaging the closeness they did have. The thought of seeing shame or revulsion on Rose's face, if Oceanna had misidentified the meaning of her warmth, somehow, miss-stepping by reaching out for her or trying to kiss her, was too heartbreaking a consideration to bear.

As close as they had become, touching had been a step too far. Rose thought she needed to be straight, whether satisfied or miserable. Now, Oceanna wondered if her "gay-dar" had blips in it, blinding her to the reason for Rose's careful distance. If there was time, maybe they could talk about it. Maybe over martinis and fried zucchini in their favorite night spot, but for now, just being on the other end of the phone would have to do.

Respectfully, the nurse signaled to Rose that it was her turn. She tucked the phone into her bra, stood obediently, and walked in the direction of the exam room. X-ray films were hanging on the light screens, her bones on display. Oceanna heard the doctor ask Rose to sit as he pointed out the areas in question.

"You see these white areas? These are normal bone, the pelvic curve, and the hip joint. This is a healthy tendon and muscle… but this mass is not normal, located in the uterus, probably a tumor. I want to biopsy it today. OK?" he patted her shoulder. "This is scary, but it is a short procedure. It feels like a bite. I'll make it fast; just put on the gown and lie down."

Tears rolled down her face. She looked at her phone, seeking support, battery dead, stuck her lifeline back in her bra, disrobed her lower parts the rest of the way and stuck her feet in the stirrups and waited.

A long metal instrument with razor-sharp scissors in the tip was inserted. The doctor patiently reminded her to relax several times. The long probe bit chunks of flesh from the effected tissue. Searing pain brought Rose to an outright scream. After apologies, the collected dark tissues were dropped into glass tubes and were marched out by the attending nurse to the lab.

Afterward, the biopsy left her feeling chewed. She filled a prescription for Oxy and one for depression, took one of each immediately, and drifted out of the hospital the way she came in, just more dazed and exhausted. She changed the pad in her pants to extra-large. The plastic liner made her crackle as she trudged through the halls, longing for home.

She tucked the dead phone under her chin, pinching it tight between her jaw and shoulder, hugging her friend in spirit, feeling the comfort of emotional support, knowing she was there, close, no matter what.

She prayed on the elevator. Hummed a Christmas tune down the stairs, felt the rain on her face at the bus stop, and stared out at the storm over the city until she got downtown. Then, she connected with the light rail going east to Lloyd Center from Pioneer Square.

She didn't feel the cold, but the large digital thermometer read thirty-eight degrees. Her hands were numb. She rubbed them together, forgetting gloves. Teenagers with bicycles rolled on the train, running over her feet. She didn't feel it, so she told them she was okay.

Getting off at her stop, she waited for the light to change, stepped off the curb in front of a turning car that blared its horn at her, she kept crossing, unflapped.

The stair rail to her door was slick and wet. She pulled herself up with blue hands. Her keys tangled in her fingers, frustrating her. She kicked the door and stabbed the key into the lock, shoved the door open, stomped in, and slammed it behind her. Rose threw the bags of pills and papers across the room and screamed with aggravation. Choking and crying, she dropped to the floor. She was freezing.

"Why this torture God? Why?" she uttered through chattering teeth.

The floor was hard. Defiantly, she kicked off her soggy shoes and tore off her socks, peeled off dripping jogging pants, waddled to the shower, and jerked her shirt off over her head, sheering off the buttons that ricocheted off the bathroom tiles with a clatter. She ripped off her stained pad and jammed it into the trash like a murderer assaulting a body. The hot water was ready at the shower head right away, billowing steam. She stepped into the tub and let the heat penetrate her back, which ached even after she took a pain pill. She took another, drinking it down with the shower spray, wishing it was wine.

Her favorite shampoo oozed smooth, glistening gel into her palm as she squeezed it, filling her nose with a soft, flowery fragrance. Washing her long hair, she massaged the suds into her scalp with her fingers, around her brow, and into her face, inhaling deeply the hot mist and perfume. She pressed firmly into her cheeks with her fingertips to relax and recover an alive feeling again.

As she focused on letting go of the tension in her back and stiff legs, her muscles gave up the anxiety, lengthening and smoothing. Blood entered and cleared away the angry grip. Her scalp tingled and seemed to lift, freeing dark thoughts, detaching her from the concerns, directing demons to float out of her head, dissipating as they rose beyond the ceiling and over the roof top. Rose meditated, refocusing, letting go of the ghoulish images ensnaring her mind and drifted.

She switched the water from the shower spray to the tub, plugged the drain with a plastic plug, and lay down for a good long soak. She pulled herself low into the tub. The water was just under her chin. Hot water trickled into her ears, muffling the external sounds of daily life, amplifying the beating of her heart and the whisper of her breathing.

The throb in her legs and back began disappearing as she gradually let go of the disaster she feared. Slowly drifting into a fantasy, unbound by normal expectations, thoughts migrated to a wistful dream of entering a dimly lit saloon with patrons in silhouette, back lit by a colorful wall of shiny bottles.

A wall of mirrors and glass shelves reflected the long stem glasses hanging over the head of the busy bar tender pouring drinks, who waved at her to come in. Candles set all about the room flickered. Her spirit lifted as she felt the rumble of a throbbing disco beat, central to the dance party within.

The base pulse vibrating through the glass dance floor flashed to the rhythm in patches of pink, lime, and cobalt blue under her naked feet. White fog rolled in from a vent under the DJ's booth. The room seemed comfortable and new. A curious spirit filled her. She felt spry and giddy. Women gathered in small groups, sitting at small round tables at the dark perimeters of the bedazzling floor. They raised their glasses, called out her name like they knew her, and clinked them in celebration as she strolled in.

The party was for her. She plopped down on red leather bean bags piled along the boundary. Rose was mesmerized by twinkling disco balls spinning high above and enjoyed the patterns in the mist; rainbow trails rolled around the room. Heavy base drums thudded, radiating vibrations through the furniture, tables, and into the drinks, making ripples through the wine on her low table. It made her laugh out loud for the first time in weeks. She felt safe and free.

The waitress in a sexy gothic dress—a leather bodice, deep cleavage, shiny black thigh-high boots, black hair, and lipstick— appeared. A lit candle on the bar tray she carried confidently over her head. She moved among the customers.

"This one's for you, darling," she smiled at Rose and winked.

"What is it?" Rose took the glass and peered in at the pink viscous drink, decorated with a strawberry and a ring of pink sugar around the rim.

"It's what you have wanted for so long," she replied, lit a cigarette pinched in her full black lips, and passed it to Rose, leaving black lipstick on the filter. Rose was stirred by tasting the flavor of her lipstick as she pressed the filter between her own dry lips, feeling like a kiss.

Rose mumbled, "Wow!"

She fancied herself not a prude, just stubbornly moral. Although, secretly, she felt flattered when women flashed eyes her way, specifically when Oceanna let admiration show.

Maintaining the boundaries between them had fallen on Oceanna, not touching too much to avoid invitation, correcting friends that suggested more was going on than just friendship. Oceanna maintained the belief that not respecting Rose's choice of straightness was as annoying and insulting as the lewd men trying to lure lesbians into sexual encounters to "straighten them out." Rose recalled that she had twinges of disappointment but had caught herself, administered appropriate self-admonishment, and prayed earnestly for forgiveness for feeling such things. Privately, she felt intrigued and torn.

"Maybe you should follow your heart?" said the waitress after reading Rose's thoughts before moving on.

Putting the drink to her lips, she smelled the strawberry and vodka and drank the entire cocktail to the last drop, sliding smoothly down her throat.

The disc jockey danced with herself in the music booth above the flashing floor. She intuitively chose the music that would inspire the dance. Energetic and exotic, cool and in control, her breasts showing through a sheer black blouse in '80s glam-rock fashion, she spun the discs. Hair in a stiff, flame-red Mohawk, spiked a foot high, festooned with stars, her green eyes lined with heavy mascara and bright purple eye shadow; the DJ timed the song transitions perfectly, matching the tempos so the dancers could revel without skipping a beat.

She pointed at Rose with long fingers and put on the song that exposed her heart. A favorite love song with lyrics repeating a passionate desire to make love all night long, carried by a heart-breaking melody with soaring violins, backed by perfect harmonies, consuming the room.

A familiar figure floated in her direction through the fog. Oceanna materialized from the atmosphere, her bare chest glowing like a sunset, rainbow light beams radiating from her head, flashing to the rhythm. Her green eyes shimmered, desire bright, gazing at Rose and floating closer.

This time, Rose explored her friend's figure, slowly following the curve of her jaw, the turn of her mouth, and her breasts mature and pendulous. Her narrow hips and stalky legs are trimmed in form-fitting, orange, velveteen bell bottoms, accentuating the lift of her fanny and the strength in her thighs.

The room is filled with melody, rhythm, and emotion. Rose lifted into the air, off the bean bags, levitating on a charm across the dance floor into Oceanna's waiting arms. Pressing herself into Oceanna, the glow from her chest soaked into her arms and breasts as well, sending thrills down her spine. Electricity, more than electricity, seemed to run through their skin into each other; when mixed, it became a combined bliss.

Connection this natural and automatic shocked Rose. To her, the forces were unavoidable and alarmingly instantaneous. But, in this corny, gauzy dream, she reconsidered the risks of joining. Tonight, they were virtual. Her desire to find love turned back on her. For years, she had resisted the pull to be open, vulnerable, and disarmed. Now, she longed to give in.

She kept her eyes closed, cradling her face in the crook of her lover's neck, feeling her way across Oceanna's body. The smell of Amber lifted from Oceanna's skin. They bobbed up and down as they floated, mid-dance floor on cool clouds of pink and blue. She followed the full curve of her breasts, fumbling with her fingers and palms, giving in to the need to pull her close and press her cheek against her. Cupping her sweet spot gently, she took nipples into her mouth and pulled. She wanted to have Oceanna inside her, thrilling her. She burned for want of touch. Rose had never felt consumed by want like this before. She realized she had been hiding from admitting her feelings from the day she met Oceanna.

She tried to open her eyes, but they locked shut. Bracing herself for the shock of looking into the eyes of a woman who loved her made her tremble. Risking looking into the soul of the woman who loved her was too hard. She froze. She was nervous to expose her heart fully, to be seen, to kiss her wide open and bring her in. She panicked; her eyes refused to open.

"I can't! I can't!" Rose screamed. Enraged, she bolted upright with such force that half of the bath water splashed over the end of the tub onto the floor.

She sputtered and hung on to the towel rack as if clinging for dear life. She looked at the walls and toilet, confirming she was actually at home. Confused and ashamed, Rose both longed for more dreams and prayed for forgiveness for longing for more than a dream. Panting, her heart pounding, her body alert and still excited, she sat still as the phone rang for the last time, and the answering machine recorded Oceanna's message.

11
Trust

In the dark, the smell of leather and perfume permeated the cedar walls of her closet hidey-hole, bringing calm to her tortured mind. Gretchen inhaled deeply, savoring the air, and curled up among her dead mother's coats, dresses, and shoes, scooping them around her into a bumpy nest of comfy garments, heels, and laces. An army of closet dolls cuddled around her, making happy comments, hoping to comfort her. They understood the routine. Inhaling her mother's scent settled her nerves, reminding her of lost loving embraces. She pulled down her mother's fleecy barn coat from the hanger above to line the nest, plush and warm, weaving several garments together for a thick pillow, and pulled a blanket over the heap and her head, deadening the noise of the knock at the door that rattled her.

Closing her eyes, hiding, still and quiet, the aura of the dark memories drifted through, casting depressing shadows. First, pretty images of innocent childhood fun clicked into view. Favorite images of playing with the dogs, romping through the yard, chasing chickens clucking sweetly in the sun. Thoughts of climbing the pasture fences to watch her father train the trotters as they lifted hooves high, clomping around the track, then, a dark agony tightened, forcing her back to the exact moment of betrayal, like a roller coaster on an inevitable track.

Gustoff had taught with love for the first six years of Gretchen's life, down to the details of how to feed and clean the animals, speaking to her with patience and pride. The farm was joyful and seemed secure, with flowery pastures protected by acres of thick woods. She was good at her chores, collecting eggs that her mother would cook for breakfast in the wide rustic kitchen. She was confident when feeding the horses and decorated walls with pictures she had painted. She sighed, recalling the easy freedom of that summer before the change.

Her thoughts roamed uncontrollably back to that day when her life shifted from a dream into a savage nightmare. A monstrous momentum dragged her closer, back to the horror. Plugging her ears and pushing herself back into the rear of the closet, disaster loomed as she approached the spectacle of that broken day that devastated her.

She recalled the ropes used in gory abuses, synching ever tighter, dragging her repeatedly through shock and guilt, leading to the bondage of shame. She clamped her eyes tight, bracing herself for the parade of cruel images that were determined to return. As always, she tried to refuse the rot the bastard had beaten into her.

At the same time, Oceanna knocked several times, trying to perform a wellness check and hoping to connect with Gretchen under more positive circumstances after leaving her in an angry stupor the last time. Trust would have to be established before she tried to discuss anything about her father's murder. She kicked herself for bringing Dad along, with his insensitive, pointed questions, triggering the shutdown that day. She tried to shrug away the self-doubt about reestablishing a healthy connection with Gretchen.

"Gretchen has obviously been through much worse than a rude conversation," she thought.

Her years of experience in social work had taught her that relationships could be repaired. Barriers sometimes gave way to strong alliances between worker and client when genuine empathy was used, if one was patient and listened more than talked.

"No one really wants to be alone," she said to Dad one night as they watched the news. "Isolation is self-preservation at its most desperate."

She stepped back and looked up at the roof. She wondered how many rooms this strange place had and thought about the conversation. "Think of the strength it would take to live alone like that," she had said in the discussion with her father. "On a farm, away from help? No wonder she wears a gun."

"I'll bet she can use it too! Maybe she's worried the murderer would return?" Dad said, "Over five hundred shots fired. Who would need to do that?" He had looked up from his drink, "Ticking time bomb?"

As Oceanna stood on the wide front porch of Gretchen's home, her finger traced the carved horse on the door in front of her and wondered if Gustoff Loves had created it.

What did he do to deserve it? She had brainstormed out loud about the possibilities.

Oceanna rolled back in her mind, the local gossip she had been able to find around in her head, trying to find a thread that tied things together enough to make sense.

By all accounts, it had been a grizzly event in a community devoted to peace. The surrounding Amish farmers were devoted to non-violence as God's mandate. These farmers believed in letting God judge and determine punishment for sins over hundreds of years with compulsive devotion. The Amish spent hundreds of years refusing to go to any war or battle or step over the line with anything lustful or prideful. They devoted their lives to radical, meticulous order, refusing electricity, music, and most modern medicines, and insisted on living with pioneer standards dating back to before the Civil War. It seemed unlikely that one of the farmers would lose control and become enraged enough to murder Gustoff, no matter his offense.

Amish had guns for hunting deer. The skills to do the shooting were there, but killing a man? Who else was involved deeply enough to deliver such a ghastly murder? Gretchen was only fifteen when he was killed; did she see the event? She had to have heard something. Blowing off five hundred rounds of ammunition from pistols and rifles must have erupted with a roar.

The snow had been cleared off the stone porch and into a wide path to the barn. She wondered what the murder spot looked like now, after twenty years. The barn's slate shingle roof peak loomed over a hundred feet high. An enormous structure painted red, it glowed against the white of winter. The hand-excavated foundation blocks were scored with the chisel marks of the craftsman's tool, three feet long and two feet thick, quarried from local sandstone. The dark oak beams framed the structure, hand-carved from ancient trunks, built to last, and beautifully topped by an octagonal cupola. The lead glass panes were framed with black iron. Crowned with a weathervane of hammered copper, the proud copper stallion, green with age, was a lean horse rearing against the wind. She lost interest in knocking on the front door and stepped off the porch to take a closer look.

After the knocking stopped, trembling in the closet, slogging through a familiar dream scape to an inevitable grief pit, recollecting sounds triggering her wicked journey, Gretchen clutched her dolls to her face, pressing their little embroidered noses into her cheeks. She tensed, recalling the echo of her mother's cries as her father took out his anger on her with his voice and his body.

It had been twenty years since Gretchen had heard the assault from a distance while she played in the barn with a nest of kittens, mewing and wriggling under their mother. Crawling over her fluffy belly for safety and warmth, she heard her mother screaming and ran to the house, panicked, wanting to help.

Triggered and full of fear, she relived the disorientation, her heart pounding as she entered the kitchen to witness her father crushing her mother's neck with his rugged hands. Slamming her with his fists. Dragging her recklessly by the neck, her long red hair wound around in his fist. She uses her curls as a handle to pull her up the stairs into the bedroom and then throws her onto the bed. He glared over his shoulder at little Gretchen, horrified, speechless, and trembling, promising her a beating as he shoved past.

Tears rolled down her red cheeks now as they did then. She clearly remembered watching her father descend upon and brutally rape her mother, hitting her with his body repeatedly, making blood come from her, while Mama's little girl stood in silent shock, powerless. That betrayal was unbelievable. Then, he turned his anger on Gretchen. Sealing her lips with emotional cruelty and savage assault, repeatedly, until blood came from her body, too.

Days after the beating, Mother had been unable to walk, her face so swollen she could not see. The veterinarian, an old friend of Gustloff's, was called to see if he could diagnose the problem. Gustoff continued to tirade, accusing her of faking, but it did not work to motivate Mother to forgive the incident or move her legs.

Doctor of Veterinary Medicine Mitt Uhglee, having invested in Loves' breeding ventures, examined his victims and looked for other ways to preserve their reputations, both his business partners and his own. He inspected the wounds and bruises on Mrs. Loves' blackened face, back, and pelvis, sewed her up with catgut, and kept his mouth shut. After all, he and Gustoff were old friends and had been covering for each other since high school. Three months later, Doc. Uhglee was called again to help his friend. He pronounced his wife dead, while Papa informed Gretchen that she was now to take her place as Mama, with all the intimate wifely duties included.

Now, in a state of flashback, Gretchen lifted her head from the pillow made of her mother's shoes, pulled the fleece-lined coat cover away from her face, and listened. Wooden heels left reddened marks on her skin; shoestrings and sole leather left imprinted shapes on her hot cheeks from the pressure of hiding her face among them. She heard the crunch of snow underfoot, someone walking in the yard in the direction of the barn. Anxiety magnified the details of the movements outside, providing important information that helped maintain her safety in her cedar nest. She had perfected her safety measures over the years of Papa's manhandling, as well as in the aftermath of the molester's slaughter.

Remaining motionless, focusing on interpreting the pattern of shuffling in the yard, she estimated the danger level. Was it a familiar pace and weight? Was it male? Sheriff? She had no friends who came to the house anymore. Neighbors sometimes fed her when she spun over to deliver brown eggs to their kitchens on her rider. She lurched into a sitting position. The barn man-door was being pulled open with a familiar scrape and squeak of the heavy hinge. They were lurking and going in.

Feeling carefully under the blankets and boxes, into the rear of the deep closet, she hunted for the metal of the long gun's barrel buried there. She stroked the well-oiled wood stock and warm steel trigger and felt some of the panic leave her. She had learned the hard way to be ready for bear.

Unaware of Gretchen's mental state, Oceanna took in the barn's perfumed air of hay and earth, must, and wood. Barn sounds were simple—the scurry of mice, the flutter of wings, the rustle of pebbles underfoot in an otherwise silent atmosphere. Daylight streaked through the spaces of weathered boards and into the small windows, dusty and cobwebbed. Like the vaults in a cathedral, the interior swooped up in a tall, open arch, in a pattern of arches, lifting gracefully to the roof in a rugged rhythm of pillars and beams. The quality of workmanship was evident. Expertise showed in wood carved to match in huge tongue-and-groove fashion and held fast by hand-carved pegs as thick as forearms, driven with mallets of oak by pioneers with wills of iron.

Oceanna shivered as her eyes traced the soaring curves and the angled windows of the cupola. The sun-streaked mist lingered, curling casually as she disturbed the stillness. It was a private world she had entered. A spirit could be felt. A quiet presence thrived under the plank skin of this barn. She could almost stroke it and speak to it. She believed it was trying to communicate with her, whispering sighing.

Along the south side of the barn were ten first-class horse stalls. Leather bridals still hung from pegs. Loops of lead lines, training saddles, and tackle sat untouched for more than a decade, grey with dust and rot.

Oceanna stepped slowly along the stalls, peering into the gates, trying the rusty latches, and examining the dry leather. Mice left dainty trails in the dust as they took bites out of saddles and gnawed on what they could find. Corn that had dropped onto the dirt floor from the feeding buckets years before had been chewed, leaving husks. Spiders had created nests spanning several feet among the frames of the stalls; carcasses of large moths hung there, trapped by the once-invisible filaments, hung fluffy with dust.

The stalls were clear of clutter, but there was no evidence of animal dung or recent use just cleaned out and left idle. She examined a red all-terrain four-by-four vehicle that looked surprisingly well-serviced, under a canvas cover, and a well-worn but functioning antique tractor in original green paint with yellow wheels and a scoop. The smell of gasoline and oil accompanied them. Tools on long handles hung along a worn tool corral. Hoses and pipes, ropes, long and of various colors, for specific functions, stored logically, rolled up, and hung for the next needed repair that would pop up. Hay bales were stacked in tightly bound blocks, with chickens clucking among them. Red hens remained on their nests as she passed by.

Oceanna shivered as her eyes traced the soaring curves and angled windows of the cupola. The sun-streaked mist lingered, curling casually as she disturbed the stillness. It was a private world she had entered. A spirit could be felt. A quiet presence thrived under the plank skin of this barn. She could almost stroke it and speak to it. She believed it was trying to communicate with her, whispering and sighing.

Along the south side of the barn were ten first-class horse stalls. Leather bridles still hung from pegs. Loops of lead lines, training saddles, and tackle sat untouched for more than a decade, grey with dust and rot.

Oceanna stepped slowly along the stalls, peering into the gates, trying the rusty latches, and examining the dry leather. Mice left dainty trails in the dust as they took bites out of saddles and gnawed on whatever they could find. Corn that had dropped onto the dirt floor from the feeding buckets years before had been chewed, leaving husks. Spiders had created nests spanning several feet among the frames of the stalls; carcasses of large moths hung there, trapped by the once-invisible filaments, fluffy with dust.

The stalls were clear of clutter, but there was no evidence of animal dung or recent use—just cleaned out and left idle. She examined a red all-terrain four-by-four vehicle that looked surprisingly well-serviced, under a canvas cover, and a well-worn but functioning antique tractor in original green paint with yellow wheels and a scoop. The smell of gasoline and oil accompanied them. Tools on long handles hung along a worn tool corral. Hoses and pipes, ropes—long and of various colors, for specific functions—were stored logically, rolled up, and hung for the next needed repair that would pop up. Hay bales were stacked in tightly bound blocks, with chickens clucking among them. Red hens remained on their nests as she passed by.

As the dust settled, her eyes watered, blurring her vision. She saw glints of brass scattered over the ground where her knees and heels had dug in. Bullet shell casings still littered the ground. The wooden gate to the stall hung crooked on one hinge, riddled with hundreds of bullet holes. Splintered wood spiked out from the holes like a porcupine's quills, bullets having gone through the wood, then flesh, and out the other side of the barn wall, creating round openings in grim patterns, letting rays of gray light come through. The poke-a-dots of light sparkled in an array of spots on the floor, like the dizzying fragments of light cast from a mirrored disco ball decorating a dance platform.

Hoof marks had been pounded into the stall walls. Bits of flesh and fur still tangled in the fibers of the wood. Black blood splattered the stall walls and up to the top rails in all directions. Oceanna envisioned the horse, in terror, kicking the walls, trampling the man, gouging the walls that now bore witness to a struggle. She envisioned panic-stricken creatures lurching to save themselves as the killer shot from outside the stall, through the gates, into the man and horse while they rushed to duck shots ricocheting through their flesh. The bullet cast-offs caught the light, showing a path from a workbench with a gun rack and shelves across the barn from the stall, giving the direction of the killer's position.

Oceanna ran her hands over the benchtop, free of dust, and calculated the number of different guns that might have been stored in the rack. There were spots for five rifles and at least ten pistols with ammunition drawers that she could still pull out. The bench wood was worn smooth from years of service. Pistol and long gun cleaning rods were organized; rags and gun oil were fresh and stored carefully for current use. From the bench to the stall, there was a clear line of sight of about fifteen feet. She knelt to examine the smooth black goo on the ground. She considered the sheer volume of body fluids that must have been spilled to fill the stall and leak under the gates, oozing over the dirt floor several feet all around, when the large barn door slid to the side, grinding on frozen rollers.

The silhouette squat, in baggy pants, a thick coat, and a shotgun gripped in one hand, appeared, breathing heavily, puffing vapor. They stared at one another for several seconds, quietly assessing the next moves.

Oceanna knew it must be Gretchen but was shocked at how much like her father she appeared. Tense and sullen, with a five o'clock shadow on her chubby cheeks and chin, Gretchen emanated a rage that was palpable from a distance. Her clothes had been her father's: a well-worn brown coat with matching pants that bunched up over her boots, making her look squashed. The tattered, broad-brimmed hat sat too low over her eyebrows, emphasizing her unblinking stare. Her mouth turned down in deep lines in a cartoonish frown. She was transformed from the innocent-looking child-woman she had been a couple of days before. She lifted the double barrels without effort, tilting at Oceanna.

"Gretchen. It's Oceanna, your worker. Do you remember me?" she said softly. She held her black-stained palms up in surrender. The smell was starting to make her feel sick again.

Gretchen stood solidly on two feet in a wide stance, swinging the gun gently, pointing the business end of the rifle in Oceanna's direction, balanced on her trigger finger.

"This is my barn," she growled and took a couple of steps toward the bloody stall. She surveyed the fallen canvas, the dust and fly confetti, the disturbed blood pool with footprints running through it, the rays of light filtering in through the shot-up walls and back at Oceanna, covered with gore paste, layers of dirt clinging to her knees, and sniffed the smell of death lifting off of her.

Just then, a rustling came from the bales of hay; a hen fluttered off her nest. Gretchen's attention moved to the sound; she began to raise the gun in that direction when several kittens romped through the spaces in the bales after the clucking bird. A protective mother cat jumped up, calling to them in short, puffy bursts in an attempt to keep them safe, her full tits swinging as she trotted. Oceanna stepped back slowly out of the line of Gretchen's focus, backing away into the darkness of the long barn, toward the man door she entered through, her heart pounding.

The eyes of the cat twinkled at Gretchen. She stretched her long back and purred, hoping to draw some pets and breakfast. The mental images holding Gretchen in a high state of self-defense dissolved a bit, relaxing her. She felt loneliness twist in her heart. A connection to a friend broke through. Tears trickled down her icy face. Her deep frown trembled as she started to weep. She set down the long gun gently and lay back among the hay and bouncy kittens, her body lurching in an overwhelming sob.

12
Got Gutz

Thick blue smoke curled out of her nostrils slowly, like anti-gravity syrup. The marijuana smoke, hot, dense, savory, rolled into and out of her lungs, over her tongue, and into her mind. She sucked in and held the smoke with ease and anticipation. Relaxing her diaphragm, she let it escape at its own silky pace. Lazy blue swirls surrounded her head like a halo, disrupted by the slightest movement of her hand or wink of her droopy eyes. She held still and let the weight of her chest push out the medicine.

"Whoever engineered this batch of bud was a genius," she moaned, watching the ethereal designs drift about the room until a smoky haze hung a foot thick from the ceiling.

Rose had been against marijuana for recreational and medical use for the longest, fearing people would become fiendishly addicted. She understood the arguments for it now, however, and had to admit it was medicine, and it was fun. After two hits, her anxiety diminished, indigestion turned to hunger, aches and pains disappeared, and her mind wandered into deeper considerations.

She hated to admit that on some important issues she found on reconsideration, she may have been wrong. An unexpected benefit of marijuana use was a relaxation of boundaries. This medicine gave her less restrained insight and slowed down her mind, giving her time to explore life's disappointments and blessings at a microscopic level. Pot transported her from defensiveness to the point of bravery, enough to allow contemplation.

Being vulnerable didn't seem as threatening when high. She could imagine new possibilities. Embrace a wider range of options. She opened up intellectually, more curious about why the world was the way it was and why she was the way she was. Why did she feel the way she did, and what brought her to this point in her life? She had to admit the church ladies were right; pot loosened one's morality.

"What a relief!" she laughed out loud to herself. She discovered she was great company.

She glanced at the silver picture frame still holding the crumpled picture of her last failed attempt at romance. Face down, his image looked down into hell, where he belonged. She kept within reach but in shame from the day she was forced to give him up after discovering he had a wife and children, an entire family that he lived with over the hill in Sandy,

Oceanna agreed to discuss him using the code name "Naughty Natashia" due to his secret spy mentality. A surprise call had come in for Rose while at her office at A.A.S. one average morning from a woman calling herself his wife, seeking to talk to his mistress, begging her to leave him alone as she was the mother of his three children. Rose had taken the surprise call while standing at her desk and fainted flat after getting the news that her worst nightmare was upon her. Oceanna had found her with the phone still in her hand, out like a light.

Looking back, Rose recalled his broad smile and the beautiful names he had for her. His charms had seemed so genuine. Fooled completely, she became deeply enamored. Speeding into fever pitch physical encounters she had never experienced before. It surprised her that she could become so open so fast. She had always been prudishly slow until "Natashia."

Head leaned back, feet up and floating on a warm, meditative cloud; she examined his best qualities. One was his gift of compliments that had strummed her heart strings so powerfully and his attentiveness to her budding exploration of sexual activities, which created a smooth path for him to her purse.

The desperate wife had found Rose's private mail and journals, keys to Rose's apartment, and silky underwear not belonging to herself. Rose's personal letters, utility bills, and bank statements had been stolen and hidden in the spare tire compartment of the family station wagon. The wife discovered them one drama-filled day while getting ready for a family picnic. She connected the dots. Rose's credit card statements matched her husband's strange disappearances. She had to try to save her marriage and was armed with Rose's phone number and address.

Innocently, Rose had let him in, trusting, believing he loved her. What a fool she discovered herself to be. How could she trust her own judgment after that? She was completely unnerved, humiliated, and ashamed. Shaken, she was left wondering if anyone would love her for the pleasure of her company. Wondering shakily if anyone should.

In response to his lies and stalking and Rose's depression, Oceanna purchased a glistening snub-nose .38 caliber Smith & Wesson with a shoulder holster and a concealed weapons license in the event Naughty Natashia should try to get back at Rose for calling the FBI and filing for a restraining order. Looking him right in the face, after discovering he had hidden listening devices, taped microphones, and cameras to Rose's mattress and lamp stands, she threatened him. Oceanna promised him bluntly that if he hurt Rose any further, she would shoot to kill and let the chips fall where they may.

A smile crossed her face, considering the look in Oceanna's eyes as she confronted Natashia. Pure flame. Her intensity and certainty had sent chills up Rose's spine. She had to admire purity like that. Her skin became goose-bumped at the thought of it. Pulling a blanket over her shoulders, she held that memory in her thoughts. The glamour of the experience remained clearly in her mind, retaining the intrigue for further exploration. It scared her to look close at it. Desiring to be honest, at least with herself, she held that feeling in her mind, letting it roll around in her gut.

What is it I feel? She pondered. Is it admiration? Respect? Devotion? Or… the real thing? She paused. "How to sort it out? Passion or longing with Natashia? Something less than love, passing?" she mumbled and asked herself, was it possible for her to love a woman genuinely? Would that be a sin? And if she did love Oceanna, she thought, and wanted to take her to her body, could being truly in-love purify it? Freeing her? Could she love God and enjoy genuine love and physical connection with Oceanna, too?

Her eyes jerked open; Rose caught herself mid-thought. She sat up, drop-jawed and sweating. She looked around the room for a moment to orient herself, panting. She caught the ashtray as it started to slip and sat motionless for several minutes. She continued to talk to herself out loud, which is a daily routine by now.

"Oh my God! Is this how it happens?" she squeaked. "I can't say it? How can I ...? I am a hypocrite! Right before my own eyes! Oh my God!"

She stood up, shuffled to the kitchen, poured a tall glass of wine, and drank it down. It steadied her. "Ok, Rose, just wait, you're alone. No one knows about this. You're in control. Act or do not act, that is the question," she reassured herself.

What shocked her was the comfortable feeling it gave her, dreaming of drawing herself close to Oceanna in every way. In fact, she felt she had to use constant effort to distance herself, watch herself, and keep from being carried into her arms by physical magnetism, becoming one with her friend.

"It has always been this way," she sighed, biting her lip. She felt an internal shift.

Stuffing a plain donut between her teeth, she poured another flute of white wine, grabbed the journal that she used for her initial rough book ideas and a soft lead pencil, and curled up on her favorite Lazy-Boy that heated up and vibrated.

She scratched her balding head, having lost her hair to chemotherapy, fingered soft blond bristles standing on the end where flowing locks had grown, and sighed, "I am going to leave this damn story behind fully finished, even if it is the last thing I do," she mumbled with resolve and began letting the thoughts and ideas flow unedited. Refusing to resist the pull of the story as it took a life of its own, "Like all great stories, they start writing themselves," she smiled and began to scribble.

13

Working Title: Like Her Head Was Cut Off!

Rose Cox

Dark streets, shifting shadows, moving figures, lurking men. Anxiety plagued Roxanne every night. On edge at every rattle or bump outside her house, she jumped at the sound of a car slowing down, fearing it was her stalker surveilling her location. Trapped and humiliated, her confidence had been worn away, stripped bare. Her worst nightmare had turned into reality.

She had exposed herself. Talking too much about her suspicions about who the Adult Action Services killer was. Now, she may pay the ultimate price. She may fall victim to his rage. Her faith was being tried now. Blunt attacks on her assertions that God makes all things happen for a reason were being waged. Did she really believe it? Or was she a shallow believer, just like the ones she had often maligned?

She was jumpy, though she heard whispers in the attic now and then. Shuffling outside the windows. The crush of gravel underfoot in the garden. Movement under the floorboards. But, when she rushed out to see, nothing. Darkness had become a torment. What kind of man could murder a coworker, cut off her head and arms, wind her body parts up in dirty shrink wrap, and toss her warm corpse in the dumpster, under everyone's nose, right on top, figuring Vernon would find it on one of his routine trash runs? An innocent like Vernon. Her unlikely hero. She felt nauseated, chilled, and confused. The murderer is likely to be the man she knew, trusted, and fell in love with.

She played with the fragrant bubbles under her chin. Steam rose from her bath so hot, it nearly scalded. She closed her eyes, trying to relax. The more she struggled against her terror, the more it clutched her like a tightening snake, patiently suffocating her. Skillfully swallowing her.

There was a firm knock at the door. Roxanne lurched to a sitting position. Water sloshed onto the floor. Bubbles flowed out to the bathroom door into the hall. She clung to the side of the tub, slippery and trembling. Yanking a towel off the rack, she excoriated her red skin briskly, threw the towel on the floor for traction, and pulled on a robe.

"Who is it?" she barked while trying to peep through the mini-blinds.

"Detective Pam Gutz, Portland Homicide, Ma'am," came a measured female voice.

"What is it?" she whimpered, her throat tightening, fighting the urge to cry.

"I am assigned to the murder at the vocational training warehouse," Gutz softened her tone, *"I need your help to catch him. He seems to be after you, too, correct?"*

Roxanne unlatched the locks that barred the door. "Come in. Yes."

Detective Gutz appreciated Roxanne's trepidation. Often, male officers resembled perpetrators in their looks and direct approach to questioning. That's why they sent a seasoned detective like Pam Gutz on this assignment. She knew the feeling, empathized with the terror and exhaustion that resulted from constant vigilance when avoiding a killer, and enjoyed personifying trustworthiness in the eyes of women in fear. Male officers often pushed their way in too aggressively, like they were holding the victim at the point of the spear. "Freudian metaphor intended," she thought.

"What have you discovered? I feel trapped," Roxanne pulled the robe around her and cinched the belt tightly. Her long blond hair was in a tangled bun on the top of her head.

She looked over the detective, noticing first her sturdy leather shoes, black leather, stylish low heels with silver side buckles in a western motif, and black business suit, well-tailored over her firm thighs and back side. A belt with a buckle, also silver and western, a saffron blouse, unbuttoned just to the point cleavage could be seen, tastefully, with a gleaming silver detective's badge hanging just below. Her hair was dark, in a sort of shag cut, feathered about her full cheeks, framing bright green eyes that flashed when intrigued and fixed on Roxanne unabashedly.

She held out her left hand to give her a business card identifying her office address and phone. She sported a silver band on her little finger, a complicated silver diving watch on her left wrist and a long silver pistol in a shoulder holster under her ample left breast.

Inviting the Detective to sit, Roxanne disappeared to get some comfortable clothes on and returned more organized and less self-conscious.

Detective Gutz pulled out a small pad of paper and a pen in a leather cover.

"I'll tell you some of what I know. I've been looking at the evidence and your exposure to the crime, looking for links. You have worked at the Adult Action Services vocational training site for five years as a supervisor for social workers. You have a positive reputation. The typically-abled and other-abled workers seem to like you very well, especially an older fellow named Vernon, who found the remains. He is unable to speak and conveys his thoughts through personalized sign language and pantomime. I have been informed that he comes around your office and likes to offer his help more often than others. He is protective of you," she smiled warmly. Roxanne nodded.

Detective Gutz continued, "Most coworkers like you. A few may like you too much, but you seem to be able to contain them. They all find you helpful and genuine, intelligent but a bit naive, romantically optimistic might be a better way of saying it."

Roxanne blushed, "Would you like a drink? Coffee?" she stood.

"Yes, that would be great," she observed her blush.

"I make it strong. Cream and sugar?" She tried not to look guilty or panicky. She turned to leave into the kitchen.

"Yes. Both, I like mine strong and sweet," she laughed, looking directly at Roxanne, "Do you feel Vernon could have done this?"

She turned with shock and gaped at the officer, "God No! Vernon is an innocent!"

"Well, then?" Gutz pushed.

"How about that lewd excuse for an Executive Director, Peter Strange!" Roxanne asserted, shuddered, and stepped into the kitchen.

She knew that statement had brought worsening trouble on herself, and she had knotted their bond and ensnared Detective Gutz right alongside. She created an intriguing puzzle for Gutz and a guilty pleasure for herself.

14

Vernon is a madman.

Alone in his assisted living apartment, he ran his clammy fingers along his hairless cheeks, focusing on the tickling over his face. He admired his spray of moles, grinning with pride at each one, his eyes roaming from dot to dot.

The safety-glass mirror had been pristine the day his case manager brought it over and hung it for him. Now, beat up and buckled, it hung crooked. He put his nose closer to his reflection, with one eye squinting like one of his cartoon heroes. Leaning in to focus, a fraction of an inch off the surface of the mirror, he passed his nose over the glass at a snail's pace, his nose tip pecking at his reflection.

He scolded the reflection's imperfections, growling and mimicking the enraged expression he watched on the wrestling show. He giggled, pointed at the dents, and uttered cryptic curses at them, spraying droplets of spit over the shiny veneer. For months after his staff had installed it for him, he felt a transformation. He imagined another world behind the mirror, filled with evil opposites to confront. He reached into the mirror in his imagination, wrestling with his own reflection and winning every fight, bettering his counterpart in each debate.

He slapped the look-a-like for daring to challenge him, threw an angry fit, crashed him down, and stomped him in bare heels until exhausted, he crawled off to the couch, satisfied. The plastic mirror bounced back, bent but not broken.

Five days a week, he prepared himself methodically for his job at the workshop, first, by fixing his thinning hair. He scrutinized the direction of his wispy mustache. He brushed the sparse strands daintily with a comb. He licked his ragged mustache hairs under his nose with his pointy tongue, fondling the tips, fixing them, and chuckling like a mischievous child. He combed his thin bangs, first to the front and then back while humming to the situation comedy themes on the TV that kept him company.

Vernon's musical interpretations punished listeners' ears. He ignored the complaints. Undaunted, he sang round vowel sounds jauntily, mumbling invented words through pink lips. Vernon hummed musical notes through his nose until, after an hour or so, he felt radiant.

He sang "Good morning, Ee-oo!" to the mirror, stiffening his long fingers into a pale fin. He strengthened his back and saluted. He squared his round shoulders and brushed them off crisply, right then left. Curling his fingers delicately, he grasped one of several unmatched drawer pulls on his dresser and tugged. Meeting with dry resistance, he jiggled the drawer. It came out an inch and then stuck unevenly in the dresser. He paused, shook his head in disappointment, and then jammed his fingertips into the narrow opening and yanked it open violently. A battalion of plastic army men rattled off the dresser top onto the floor. He snapped a nod victoriously and giggled.

He dug for his favorite T-shirt in the top drawer from the tangle of lesser ones, found it, and whipped it on over his head, mussing his part. After admiring himself festooned in a shirt with the Warrior Princess, thrusting her sword aloft, battle-ready, he roared pridefully and bowed to her.

Grabbing yesterday's jeans from the coat hook, he checked the lumpy pockets, making sure the daily essentials were crowded in their rightful bundles. From the right pocket, he pulled bundles of business cards he collected from people in the community: shops he liked to patrol, the minute mart where they gave him free coffee, police officers who gave him rides home when he got lost, and the social workers who supported him.

Stacked in no particular order, he tenderly pet their worn edges, turning their logos in circles below his good eye. With no ability to read, he correlated the people's identities with the decorations or logos. He became familiar with the shape of signatures and the peculiarities of the handwriting. Vernon appreciated the value of some letters, like the striking shape of the "V" in his own name. Cautiously, he drew each dog-eared rectangle close to his eyelashes and flicked the blond hairs over them, then becoming engrossed and drifting into a meditation, concentrating on the itchiness it created at the root. He studied each card's creases, thumbed textured edges, and pictured their faces. He smelled some cards; with others, he rubbed their embossed surfaces against his lips.

He rolled his eyes fiercely at the Super Rangers collectible cards and wistfully smelled the gum perfume still clinging to them. He snarled back at his favorite Wrestle Maniac card depicting Russia, an unusually muscular woman in glistening black, skintight armor, slamming a masked opponent to the mat. He smiled warmly and winked both eyes at her simultaneously. He kissed his favorite workshop friend's card, Rosy Cox, good morning, returned it to the top of the stack, and pocketed them all gingerly.

He twisted the pants to the pocket on the left side. Knowing something would stab him, he rammed his fist bravely into the pocket, lumpy with booty, dense as a rock with plastic action figures, coins, and dice.

He railed at it, sputtering through slippery lips. Then, shutting down into stealth mode, he ducked his head, looked over his shoulders, checking for critics, then closed his eyes and took a deep breath. Pulling the jeans up to his cheek, he tried hiding behind the belt loops coolly. He dipped into the mysteries of the pocket, clamped fingers around a plastic leg, and in one lightning move, yanked a figure up and out and flung it to the floor.

Attempting to maneuver a ninja spin kick, his arthritic knees refused to flex, producing a clumsy sideways lurch that toppled him into the dresser, spilling his aftershave and scattering his rusty nail collection onto the rug. With theatrical flair, he recovered his equilibrium and returned to getting dressed.

Vernon placed four red Jell-O cups, a bag of corn chips, and an applesauce into his bent lunch box and snapped it shut with a pop that made him grin. He repeated it several times until he had to scold the latch for almost making him late. He grabbed five quarters off the windowsill and made tracks for the bus stop.

He clung to the metal stair rail with both hands and took each step one at a time, protecting his lunch box by stuffing it into the front of his pea coat. He concentrated on the placement of each foot, careful not to step on his untied shoelaces as they dragged under his gum soles.

He clicked his tongue and muttered rolling sounds during the descent, his palms stinging from the chilled metal handrail. He sniffed one chapped palm, scowled, and sidestepped down the sidewalk, humming to the tune of the last TV show he had heard.

Ambling to the bus stop, leaning decidedly to the right on bowed legs, he spanned the four blocks to a tiny grocery across from the bus stop. His joints creaked with a sandy grind that Vernon tried to hum to. He strummed his fingers in and out of the holes in the wire mesh fence and growled back at the dachshund tied to a porch along the way.

Reaching the store, he peeped a greeting sound at the worn but attractive girl with crooked teeth behind the counter. He let her assist him in filling his coffee cup, as she insisted on doing, so that the sugar made it into the coffee instead of all over the countertop.

She smiled at him. "Watch out for those teenagers out there, Honey! A bunch of 'em were teasing Mike when he got off the bus yesterday. I thought there would be a fight right there. That Mike can't help it. I think it's his mean face and cussing that provokes 'em."

Vernon balled up his fist. Sneering at the described familiar situation, empathizing with her frustration, he popped his P's and batted his eyes in stern agreement. He gripped her upper arm and squeezed it to get her attention, making sure she looked him in the eye; then, pointing out the window at the bus stop, he touched a thin finger to the tip of his narrow chin and shook his head.

Not sure of the correctness of her interpretation of Vern's pantomime, she sighed heavily, capped his to-go cup, and folded the sip strip back to allow just a little drink at a time, the way he liked it.

"Vernon, you be careful, all hundred pounds of ya!" she said.

He leaned in close to her face, looked hard at her crossed teeth and red gums, smelled her smoker's breath, and then balked dramatically at her lack of confidence. Clinching her arm tight in his right hand, he gouged his left hand into his left pocket and emerged with a clenched fist, armed with three little Super Ranger action figures with just their helmeted heads in rainbow colors, spiking out between each curled knuckle, and shook it in the direction of the bus stop, dangerously.

"Vernon, you gonna save us with a fist full of doll heads?" she asked.

Gurgling, growling, and making a ferocious face, he tucked the fist, bristling with heads, under his nostrils and eyed her through them like a boxer readying his fists for a fight.

"You're gonna hit 'em with that? Like brass knuckles?" she smiled warmly, reaching her unencumbered handout. She cupped his plastic weapons tenderly. He nodded at her dark smile.

"Well, Super Vernon, they'll never see it coming. To thank you, I'm giving you a peanut butter cup… free!" She lifted a bright package off the display and dangled it in his face.

Vernon snatched the treasure from her and scurried to the glass bus shelter, concealing the candy in his rear pocket before he got within smelling distance of Mike, who stood brooding in the corner of the glass structure, as usual.

"Well . . . Vernon, you got coffee?" Mike whispered in a thirsty, low breath, "And sugar?" He hissed.

Vernon nodded.

"And . . . cream?" He turned his rugged face to see and rolled his eyes, following Vern out of the corner of his heavy lids. Fluffy eyebrows and deep-set sockets made Mike's gaze intense and seem threatening even when he was happy. He spoke through clenched teeth, rippling the thick muscles along a square jaw.

Vernon nodded.

"Give me a taste, Vernon, old buddy?" Mike requested with an implied violence.

Hugging the cup close to the lunch box under his coat, Vernon turned his shoulder to Mike, stuck out his tongue, and shook his head defiantly.

"What? Are you accusing me… of wanting to steal?" Mike roared a laugh, throwing his head back, his wide jaw dropped full open, giving a deep vista down his throat to red tonsils. He sidestepped along the wall to Vern's end, leaned forward, looming tall over him, diminishing Vern to a midget status, and panted into his face. One bloodshot eye bulged, focusing to the right, the other to the left, down at Vernon. Restraining rage through clenched teeth, he dared confrontation, "Is that . . . nice?"

The back of Mike's coat started to rip from the force of his fists straining down into his pockets, stretching the plastic of his raincoat like two anvils, distending with the force of gravity. His voice reverberated around the enclosure through Vernon's head, rattling his eardrums. He covered one ear with his free hand, shook his head, and returned an eye-bulging stare of his own.

"Do you think I'm gonna . . . snap your skinny neck . . . for a lousy cup of coffee . . . with your spit in it?" Mike wedged himself in, pressing Vernon tightly into the dusty corner of the glass shelter, and mocked in a low whisper, "That's inappropriate!"

"Hey jack asses, what's going on?" A familiar sarcastic voice blurted from the curb behind Mike's broad back, immobilizing him.

The skinny teenager brushed his long curls out of his eyes, pulled out a filterless cigarette from its colorful box, jammed the flip top shut, stuck the pack in his front jeans pocket, and lit it with a tall flame from a square silver lighter, all in one smooth movement. Smoke raced out his greasy nose.

"It's just the fatty and skinny show! They don't have money for taking," a second boy gallantly smirked and flipped Vern and Mike the middle finger. The chubby girl with large breasts he was trying to impress giggled.

"You mean dumb and dumber?" said the first boy after spitting on the sidewalk.

"Don't overestimate these geniuses," said the second, "A terribly wasted mind is a terrible thing to . . . have!" He made a thick sucking sound.

"No worries. These queers don't have a single mind between them," replied the first.

"It takes one to know one," the girl teased, flipping her long hair over her shoulder and showing a dirty bra strap.

Mike and Vernon looked into each other's eyes silently, Vernon's face hidden from their view by Mike's girth. Mike's face was hidden by his turned back, and his broad gaping mouth breathed anxious wind into Vernon's hair, tousling it and tickling his forehead.

Twitching bony shoulders, Vernon wriggled to increase the space between their chests, clucking his tongue in a secret code. He pushed his palm against Mike's anxiously heaving sternum and felt the ramming of his heart. Mike took a step back but continued to face the rear wall, keeping his sweating back to the kids, and sidestepped back to the unoccupied end of the shelter.

Misty rays of morning sun struck Vernon's cheeks; he squinted. The ache of his pupils contracting made him yelp. He covered his eyes with his bent elbow and coat sleeve. The kids tittered.

"What's the matter, freak show, you a vampire too?" The first boy spat again, then mumbled, "Retard."

Stiffening his back, Vernon set his coffee on the bus bench, struggled to keep the lid from popping off, and cocked his coat collar up on the end around his neck. He tripped, attempting to jump into a broader, heroic-looking stance. Bending his elbows with a snappy up-and-out jerk, he created the look of fragile wings. Then he balled up both fists, rested them on his narrow hips, and stood proudly, flaring his nostrils at the teenagers.

They laughed and said he looked like a beached carp. He worked his thin lips and thick tongue effortfully, trying to form words in retort, but no sound emerged.

"Maybe he's having a seizure?" The girl taunted, rolling her eyes.

"Or, maybe… he wants to kiss you!" Yelled the second boy, hoping to get the girl's attention and inspire her interest in himself.

Responding, at slow speed, Vernon delivered a jolting "Ahhhh-Ha!" in a high cry that shook the glass walls, bouncing off the bus shelter like a trumpet blast.

The girl's head jerked back in surprise. She grabbed her own neck, squealed, faked a retch, and exaggerated a stagger down the sidewalk in an attempt to regain her feminine dignity.

Vernon remained poised and posed, feet widely stanced, fists on hips, elbows out, and his pink lips stretched into a ludicrous grin. He rolled his eyes back into his head in an attempt to look at the sun, but his eyelids kept fluttering, blocking his view.

Mike clinched his jaw and continued showing his back, compressed into the far corner, wringing his hands fitfully and mumbling rudely to himself, "Something-something Vernon" and "something-something cops" and "something-something bullshit!"

The boys sputtered, slapped their knees, and entertained themselves, mimicking the "freaks," laughing until they cried.

Vernon's undersized nostrils pulsated, eyes batted speedily, watering at the sun. He reached for his arsenal by first shooting both hands up into the air like an Olympic gymnast signaling readiness to begin, arms rigidly straight, hands flat, in line fingers fused firmly, one finger against the next, and his mouth twisted maniacally in a bright snarl, turned up at one end. As a warning, he whipped one hand down and pointed at his left front pocket, bulging chunkily, and rolled his R's like a bullfrog.

Mike, alerted by the fast movements, half-stepped in a circle to face them. His face reddening under pressure, a psychotic smile uncoiled across his rugged face. He growled like thunder, "Are ya gonna . . . kill 'em, Vernon?"

The first boy fell to his knees, overcome by convulsive cackling. He held his stomach and coughed up soda pop, which sprayed out and extended from his nose in long strands to the pavement. He grimaced. Lurching with each guffaw, gasping for breath in between, his body lay clinched in a curl.

The second boy winced and tore at the front of his pants with white knuckles, yelling, "Stop! Stop! I'm gonna wet my…," but it was too late. A yellow puddle was spreading down his pant leg to his brand-name basketball shoes on its way to the gutter.

Vernon rounded his grip into a formidable claw, kissed it tenderly, and entered his left front pocket with the tip of his fingers, feeling for tiny heads, hands, and helmets, knowing the shapes one from another until he knocked into the ones he sought and closed on them.

He whipped each glowing Super Ranger out, one at a time; one, two, three, fit them between his fingers, up against the web of his palm, and clutched them into place.

On the ground, the boys lay sweating, legs pulled up to their chests, gasping for air, showing off in adolescent drama, attracting attention as much as possible. Pimpled brows, slick with sweat, trickles of brine rolling into their eyes, stinging them blind. The girl ran down the street yelling that this was why she did not hang with retards.

Vernon stepped forward and pressed the doll's heads deeply into the first boy's hairless pimpled cheek. The boy struggled onto his knee, attempting to run after the girl, but he was dragged through his friend's urine puddle. The smell of it further deranged him, and his laughter increased into agonized convulsions. He collapsed and begged for mercy as part of his psychodrama.

Later at work, Vernon was reprimanded for putting shirts on hangers, on all the rolling racks inside-out and backward, so that the satin tags stood up defiantly. He bobbed his head and grinned while standing too close to his pretty-smelling job coach as she explained the correct way to hang shirts for the tenth time.

During lunch in the Adult Action Services' cafeteria, Vernon batted his eyes at Mike as he acted out the retelling of the morning's situation, struggling to get a group of doubtful coworkers to believe his frenzied portrayal of Vernon's superpowers during the morning's events. They looked at Vernon. They looked at Mike. They shook their heads at each other.

Vernon admired Mike's grisly bulging eyes, sweating neck, deep rocky voice, and lips pulled tight across his gritting teeth, jowls jostling, and meaty forearms with thick and pulsating veins. He giggled and grinned at Mike's show while enjoying the cool smoothness of red Jell-O sliding down his throat.

He felt unconcerned at the coworker's eye rolls and tongue-clucking. He found it hard to boast. He ignored the urge to feel disappointed about being underestimated by his friends. He just wanted to feel good. The beauty of his survival strategy was in its elegance anyway. Vernon had stumbled onto something essential. He figured out that to leverage life toward fulfillment, you must know where and when to place the fulcrum.

15
Broken Hearts

Oceanna listened to her most recent chapter entry on the recorder, leaning back in her desk chair, rocking and squeaking, eyes closed, listening for rough sentences that distracted her from the flow.

"Did you kill Candice Jam?" the Fat Cop tried to stare a hole through her across the metal table.

"Hell no," Yvonne replied.

"Was she your lover?"

"Yes, and I was in love with her, deeply."

"You felt passionately about her. Was your relationship... open? Did you have sex with... other ladies?" the Old Cop inquired.

"You straight cops are quick to bring up this fantasy," Yvonne scoffed. "Yes, she acted on her impulses. Our relationship was new. It happens with younger women."

"What do you mean, 'It happens'?" the Old Cop pressed.

"Look at her picture," Yvonne said. "She attracted a lot of attention. She was widely admired, shall I say. She danced... empowered, she liked getting looked over. I loved looking at her and... I loved her."

"She stripped at the Leather and Feather Club, right?" the Fat Cop interjected.

He flipped through a binder with plastic pages holding the crime scene pictures as well as before and after shots of Candice. He had collected promotional shots of her that had been displayed on the club billboard: glamorous handmade costumes, each one a work of art. He lingered on the one of her straddling a pole, bare-bottomed, sporting black leather chaps and a white feather boa, her long red hair just covering her nipples. He passed it to his partner, who smiled and then slid it under Yvonne's nose, seeking a reaction.

"Did you think about killing her?" the Fat Cop asked.

"Oh sure... daily!" Yvonne remarked sarcastically.

"How did you want to kill her? I mean, by what means, you know?" the Old Cop inquired.

Oceanna shook her head. The dialogue was rotten. She struggled to relax and let it flow, struggling not to struggle. She walked away from the screen, wondering why on earth she had ever wanted to create a book! She thought the story would come into her head and follow a consistent flow that could be captured and written down simply. This was torture! She thought she had a chapter, a piece of the story in her head, but as she wrote it, it seemed to get tangled, and what seemed good one moment seemed ridiculous the next. Putting several chapters together in an organized whole felt like jamming ideas together, leaving her unsatisfied.

"Where the hell is Rose?" she grumbled. She hadn't called in a week.

The dialogue felt old and tired. Rose contemplated what it would be like to be grilled for murder after losing the woman she loved in such a horrific way, her satin body reduced to blisters and charred remains. How could you get through it, being blamed for the wretched event? Would this character lose her train of thought, give in to the stress, and inadvertently incriminate herself? Was she guilty on some level? How does one endure after an event like the murder of Gretchen Loves?

Gretchen was clearly broken, tortured, and isolated after the horrible loss, but before, how was she? What was her life like as a child? Was it the loss of loving relationships with her parents when Gustloff was murdered? And what happened to her mother? Maybe both were killed in the barn—God knows there was enough black mud and flies that could have been made by another body leaking.

Dad snorted and mumbled a few words. His head lolled back, feet raised in his recliner in a deep sleep. She found herself staring at him, wondering what it would take to drive her to kill her father.

"What would he have to do to make me kill him?" she thought out loud. "What assault? What intensity of mistreatment would he have to deliver to make killing him feel right?"

She considered being beaten. The details of being hit and smashed, emotionally tortured, isolated, or raped were almost impossible to hold for very long in her mind. She found herself avoiding the images.

"What if you had to look at it daily? What if you were haunted by horror and could not escape the recurrent visions?" she said to herself. She started to feel foggy; her head was refusing to think about it. She began to nod off in her chair when, just a moment ago, she had been bright.

I have to slog through this? she thought. "I have just to push through, or this story will never finish." She pulled the rocker up and met the keyboard on the desk with trepidation. "How can it be so hard to include made-up drama into a story? I feel sadness cutting me off."

She shook her head and cracked her back, which had stiffened and knotted up. Her eyes wandered over to her calendar with the scribbled meeting dates and times she had for work. "Gretchen Loves home visits at noon, a week from today. That'll be another loo!" she mumbled, both dreading the face-to-face and being enticed by the puzzle.

Fat Cop: "...you worked at the bar together? Right?" He stared at the pictures and wrote little notes with his cheap black pen.

Yvonne: "Yeah. I am the DJ on all featured nights. The ladies chose their music. We practiced the entrances and cues, so I would have the right music ready and cued up, ready for the performances. That's how we met. I have a special way of tempo matching, you know, beat matching that is seamless. I fade in and out as part of the dancer's presentation. Costume changes and stuff."

Old Cop: "So, you watched all the other people look at your girlfriend? Give extra tips and all? That sounds tough... watching all the winks, and maybe some favoritism to a patron aggravated you? It seems like you would be pissed off and ready for a fight after a night of that."

Yvonne: "Yeah, well, that's you. If you ever fall for a performer, you must give up the thought of owning them. They are visions. They share their guts with the audience. Dancing frees the dancer. Showing their vulnerability turns them on... if you really love that kind of woman, you have to be in love with seeing her shine."

Fat Cop: Smiling a vulgar grin, "So, you are a professional couple. You do this—watching her dance naked in front of others— and you never get jealous. Okay. We've got witnesses saying that you fight, too! They were described as brawls by a couple of female patrons. So, all was not perfect or laid back?"

Yvonne looked at the pictures of charred walls, smoke billowing up, flames being beaten back by forceful water hoses, and firemen leaning into the danger. She had fallen for Candice with no effort, just got captured by the glint in her green eyes, the thrilling world that was her body, and the depth of her conversation. She was passionate about her dancing, her costumes, and her drama. Not only was Candice inspiring to look at, but she was enchanting, always fascinated with the experience of being genuine, vulnerable, and exposed, feeling unbound, like flying. Yvonne had wondered if too much exposure would eventually destroy or elevate her.

Yvonne: "She was a white-hot spirit, boiling over. She was so driven to find her bliss, her core, and refused any reasons to hide. She hated stopping short; she was all in. I worried about her, and we did fight about that. She brought out the best in me. I was part of her journey. I got selfish and star. I needed her, and I have refused to need anyone before. I felt open and vulnerable and strong at the same time. It was scary tried to control things. I didn't shine as brightly; she was the."

Old Cop: "So maybe you got too scared?"

Fat Cop: "Who else could have done this? It took hate."

Yvonne: "She was really kind of perfect in an impulsive kind of way. I envied her freedom... her daring. Whoever killed her is a beast."

She put her head down and closed her eyes out of sight of the interrogators. She tucked her face to recall the privateness of her feelings for Candice. The horror of the murder and the unimaginable situation of being accused of killing her.

The words crawled onto the page like three-legged ants, grotesque and in-artful. Gloppy phrases jammed up in her head, frustrating her, making Oceanna feel like passing out, blacking out. It was a strange reaction to the story; she had felt driven to write, but now, her feelings were turned inside out by the clumsy storyline.

Where is this path taking her anyway? she thought. It felt like the tale was moving in a direction on its own. It seemed like the story was guiding her rather than the other way around. The characters were not being drawn out by the author. Rather, the characters were claiming the conversation on their own.

She felt sick to her stomach and heavy-headed. Her brow knitted, racked with anxiety, and her thoughts rolled on. The desire to run filled her. An urgent need to get up and run out of the house, down the street, and fade into the forest filled her. But why? The desire for every muscle to ache as a happy distraction seemed ridiculous. Why? She wanted to escape… from what?

Dad pulled the recliner lever, lowering his feet. He had to go. Oceanna stood up from her keyboard, pulled Dad from his chair, and clanked along with him, clinging to the walker on the way to the porcelain. Even dealing with her father did not dislodge her mind from the story. Foggy in the head, she moved through their evening routine; finally, he was in bed with the rails up, pills down the hatch, and quiet. Now, she had no excuse not to continue the chapter. She poured a drink.

She felt she was being haunted, muses whispering in her ears, channeling the moods of real spirits through some supernatural corridors. Her mind was filled with images and conversations in another world; they really seemed to matter.

"But these people are fake!" she shook her head. "I make them up, not actual!" She stared at the keyboard. The personalities piloted the story, taking over somehow. "Maybe it's the isolation?" she thought. She felt detached, living apart from the embrace of her Portland world with just her father and the likes of tortured beings like Gretchen.

Again, she thought of Gretchen. The smell of the barn floor. The grizzly, tacky sand and scent that had clung to her skin for days after she had scrubbed it away. The deep, dark passion in that poor girl's dilated eyes and the experienced grip she had on the gun in her hand.

How did people write books anyhow? she thought. Especially the long ones, the trilogies, without going mad. Crap, what dungeon-level depression would that bring to write those things! She drank the wine and poured another immediately. Rubbing her eyes and bracing herself with a sigh, she continued.

Yvonne felt the press of the cold metal table on her brow as she leaned face down, finding it refreshing. The heat of her thoughts and the uncomfortable chair punished her. "I deserve punishment," she thought. "For not loving her better and not telling her."

Yvonne: "I held back my feelings. That was my real crime," she said flatly to the floor. "I could have been a better friend and lover, it's true. I should have let go and been... honest."

She almost smiled, recalling their first date. Candice had called unexpectedly, late one night, announcing she wanted company for the night, asking if Yvonne could bring a soft rope and good vodka with her in an hour.

Still dressed in her pajamas, Yvonne had raced to the all-night market, her heart pounding with anticipation. She jogged to the hardware aisle, seeking the braided, super soft nylon rope often used for bondage because it did not chafe. The rope was there, a-plenty, on a thick reel, but the hot cutter, meant to melt the end of nylon rope to prevent fraying, was missing. Her eyes scanned for quick options. Twenty minutes had passed already.

She found a package of fish carving knives on the sports shelves, tore open the package in a frenzy, cut off twenty feet, and stepped quickly to the liquor department. On the way, she passed the flowers. A bundle of perfect, pale, long-stem roses called to her from the cold case. They were the same pale, luminous color as Candice. She pulled them from their stand, loaded them into her cart, and continued speedily. The wheels spun and clattered as she zoomed along the aisles.

The line was long when she made it to the cashier. Her cart was filled with lovelies: wine, vodka, a dozen white roses, strawberries dipped in chocolate and a twenty-foot length of satin rope. She stood panting behind a woman holding two small children with a load of diapers and stacks of canned milk in her cart.

The young mother turned around to look behind her, curious about the heavy breathing and met eyes with Yvonne. She scanned her unusual shopping attire: black satin pajamas dotted with peace signs and little red hearts, dark mussy hair sticking up here and there in cowlicks, the vodka, wine, and rope, sniffed the roses, and smiled.

"First date?" She asked with a lilt and a pink blush.

"Oh . . . yes!" Yvonne grinned and blushed back.

"Well, I don't want to delay you. Please, go ahead of us," she said, stepping aside to let her at the cashier ahead of them.

The date had been thrilling, passionate, slow, and candlelit. Their eyes for each other were luminous like the moon. Candice took time with her kisses. Her lips intoxicated her lover, drifting them off into private universes, dislodging them from previous limits or explanations, making room for feelings to swell and desire to share. Their skins glided over each other, causing sparks in their heads and bodies. The ropes were tied loosely and lovingly around slender wrists. Rushes of excitement filled them as hands and hips rubbed across each other.

Yvonne slipped her fingers deep inside Candice. She responded with gushes of hot nectar. Candice rolled Yvonne onto her belly and pressed her breasts into her back, penetrating her with a fat phallus, quickening her push and pull until she reached her limit. Candice screamed and shuddered and plopped down face-first into the pillows, sweating. Together, they were phenomenal.

The words stopped coming. Her thoughts were of Rose, the look of her hair on pink cheeks after a good laugh and a glass of wine. The turn of her smile and the blue of her shining eyes drew Oceanna in. She tried to call again. No answer.

16
Pumpkineers!

Orange and yellow leaves fluttered on gusts of wind, crackling dry against each other as they shed from ancient Maples and Oaks in densely wooded acres surrounding the local fall festival. Eclectic enthusiasts crowded into the church parking lot and descended in bunches into the traditional Huntsburg Pumpkin Festival.

The wide octagonal gazebo glistened at the center of the doings, decorated in Halloween favorites: plastic skeletons dancing and very large Jack-o'-lanterns grinning with jagged teeth, carved by the local elementary school kids. The giant gourds they had grown occupied the center of the event. The pointed roof of the gazebo lit up with wire webs of lights in fall colors and enormous paper long-legged spiders poised to strike, swinging madly in the crisp blusters.

Heavy clouds tumbled over each other in the sunset skies, threatening a storm, broiling gold and grey on the horizon. American flags fluttered, and banners waved, festooning the rolling, shaggy fields and islands of mowed event areas of fairgrounds. Golden sunset streaks shot through the low clouds periodically as they tumbled overhead. Lightning flashed and thunder grumbled in the distance as the competing pumpkin growers lugged their thousand-plus-pound pumpkins to the scales on flatbed wagons pulled by roaring tractors for the judges to weigh and measure. Each farmer lovingly cherished their grotesque gourds, hoping for the first prize money.

Parading antique tractors, restored and painted with fresh but original colors, chugged along the gravel paths throughout the fairgrounds. Proud mechanics bouncing in the high drivers' seats, pulled fluffy hay wagons for children to ride on, rolling over serpentine paths through the haunted forest, set with spooky, jump-out ghosts and zombies rife with gore, manifested by the giddy Huntsburg High School drama club.

The acres of graves in Huntsburg Cemetery bordered one end of the fairground, packed tight with genuine tombs marked with tipping headstones of actual frontiersmen and women, Civil War heroes, and Underground Railroad volunteers, giving authenticity to the presence of spirits at the carnival. Graves dating back to 1799, when Huntsburg was founded, lay in rows over soft meadows behind the Church of Christ's Bible study group's vegetable garden, ending at the thick trunks and tangled roots of the Haunted Hundred Acre Woods. It is the only thrill ride at the fair.

The grave markers, eroded by decades of rain and snow, leaned in different directions, giving the cemetery a lively look, as though the spirits were churning, digging their way back to a swig of whisky or to grab partyers daring to trundle over them, disrespectfully. Tiki torches blazed, fluttering along the dirt alleys lined with booths and placed along the paths to the competition sites and into the woods to provide golden guiding lights, marching out into the darkness, giving warmth and direction to patrons in the brisk evening atmosphere.

Vendors stood behind their wooden displays of homemade pies and bread, pumpkin and apple pastries, fruit baskets for holiday tables, and hand-woven cornucopia horns for Thanksgiving settings. Old Amish women in their traditional white bonnets and compulsory handmade frocks, styles unchanged for the last five hundred years, folded naturally into the population of Civil War re-enactors in Union and Rebel costumes. While they knitted hats, scarves, and sweaters and chatted with each other, sharing local gossip and negotiating prices, they giggled. Wide, hand-sewn quilts hung on high frames. Floral patterns in soft colors had price tags of $500 and up.

Hot apple cider carts steamed and smelled of cinnamon. Mist rose from their fake cauldrons as grizzly ghouls stirred the brews. Pale plastic skeletons lit with torches, posed in active scenes under the trees with large jack-o'-lanterns carved at their feet, populated the grounds. Hundreds of ghostly faces cut into enormous pumpkins glowed yellow, flashing broad grins and grimaces dotting the paths around the dusk-gray acres, shimmering over the rolling pasture to the edge of the woods.

As a tradition, a band played on the gazebo, featuring Dotty Pax and The Pumpkineers. The rasp of Dotty's husky voice filtered through the evening; couples rocked and danced at the edge of the stage while delicious aromas of hot dogs and roasting pretzels filled the evening breeze. Dotty sang sweet country love songs, some known, some original. Her band thumped along with easy precision while the slide of the beautiful fiddlers' fingers broke your heart with perfect harmonies.

Children marched in their best costumes in front of a gaggle of judges, hoping to win the first prize. Werewolves and witches scuffed along, carrying pillowcases heavy with candy, giggling and barking at each other. Teenagers tried to trick the old men and buy beer at the Haunted Barn Bar and Raffle Stand. Boys attempting to disguise themselves with gray grease paints, becoming stoop-shouldered zombies with wax wrinkles and moldering soldier uniforms, called out brand names at the counter, but the bartenders recognized them as members of the Huntsburg football team and teased them back. Disappointed, the ghouls trotted off to smoke pot in the blue shadows.

Civil War costumes sewn with attention to original detail were worn by the local ancestors of the Civil War heroes during battle reenactments on one end of the rolling lawn. Restored long guns leaned in pyramid bundles, ready for battle. Some rusted bayonets were rumored to have Rebel blood still on them. Ladies in hoop skirts and bonnets swung as they prepared food on the bonfires and sipped hot ciders and wine, while their men folk wore uniforms and gathered in groups to brag, sharing their rifle shooting techniques and delighting in their cannons. Their shifting silhouettes, dark against the sunset, seemed to float like returning ghosts on the horizon, celebrating one gay night of feasting before curling up for a long sleep back in their cold crypts.

Oceanna rolled the Jeep up behind the Classic Car Club's display parking lot as Dad pointed out the spot. He got the front row slot, given to Jack Pontiac, as an honor each year, assigned by his veteran comrades who spent the winter months restoring to mint condition old rusty heaps, then, brimming with pride, as they drove the flashy classic cars in the parade.

Rows of manicured classics glistened in the tiki lights, among them an original yellow Super-bee, a baby blue Cutlass with black interior, a Ford Mustang with a black racing stripe down the middle of the hood, showing a rearing mustang hood ornament, a Hot Rod modified from a 1940s coupe, bristling with exhaust pipes radiating from a chrome-plated engine, and a red Studebaker pickup with a black leather bench seat and red and black fuzzy dice hanging from the rearview mirror. Dad had stuck his trademark magnetic flashing red emergency light on the hood and located the yellowing Los Angeles Times press card on the dash, giving them a parade-ready look.

This Halloween, Dad dressed proudly in his red plaid coat and World War II pilot's cap with several medals identifying him as a chapter member of the club, with his old rank and type of bomber he had piloted sewn on.

Oceanna wore one of Dad's black silk work jackets, his white dress shirt and 1960s narrow black tie from back in the day, a fake mustache, and Dad's black Fedora with an original, now crumpled and yellowing, press ID card stuck in the band, just like he had done for thirty years.

The Vets waved at Dad with a whoop and shook silver whisky flasks at him as an invitation to join them in their smoke, drink, and chatter. They hugged Oceanna and commented on her appearance, teasing her that she had never looked better. They also helped "Jack the Bomber" climb out of the Jeep. Delicately, they guided him into a rugged wheelchair with fat tires made for rough terrain and wheeled him over to their gathering spot with a small bonfire and lawn chairs.

Since Dad was comfortable and occupied, Oceanna was ordained to take the annual pictures of the festivities for the local newspaper, affectionally called the Huntsburg Harold, promising to share the byline with her father. His instructions were to get the faces of the children, reaction shots of the faces of the participants as they revealed the winner of the Biggest Pumpkin Contest and the Best Costume and the Pumpkin Princess in her fairy dress and crown riding in her pumpkin chariot. Oceanna looked forward to that.

Dad's trusted Pentax 1000 around her neck, loaded with the right 35-millimeter film for low light and a zoom lens for taking tight close-ups at sixty feet, pockets bulging with spare rolls of film, she wandered off to capture the party.

She strolled down the grassy corridors of booths, framing the participants in her lens's cross hairs. Stalking from a distance, she captured warm interactions, smiles, and souls reaching out to each other, inviting friendship while she remained uninvolved, like a peeping tom intruding in secret. The illusion of being close was compelling. A simple kind of relationship developed with no demands. She could imagine she was interacting while escaping any messy burden or responsibility. She could study lovers and even pretend she was one of them. As she drifted anonymously among the community of friends and neighbors, she gained insight into her father's devotion to photography. He could love his subjects and feel gloomy or bright with them while remaining selfishly private. No, give or take, that may be inconvenient.

The balance of the camera box and lens felt comfortable in her hand. The chemical smell of the film, the slide of the shutter, the sweep of the wind lever, seductive. She ducked in and out of the groups of children singing "trick or treat" for drops of candy into their sacks as they rousted the booths for sweet booty. Snap, wind, snap. She caught glee in the eyes of the goblins while they showed off and satisfaction in the smiles of the growers as they patted their enormous pumpkins, set them on the grand produce scale to prove the heaviest, and measured them for the roundest. Proud pumpkin parents congratulated each other on the weeks of doting and devotion it took to encourage their seedlings into giants. She framed the shots as tightly as she could while determining the context of the situation.

She had to hop quickly to dodge the Pumpkin Princess as she rattled up at a fast trot, elegantly wrapped in her translucent green gown, dashed with orange sparkles. Her skirt rustled and flashed. A flowing orange cape fluttered on her back. She had tall black cowboy boots on her feet, a steep rhinestone crown with the words "Huntsburg Princess" in glittering rhinestones, and orange foil gloves up to her elbows. She rode tall, standing on a wooden chariot decorated with corn stalks, scarecrows, and battery-powered jack-o'-lanterns, grinning with holiday spirit, pulled by twin black ponies, outfitted with silver unicorn horns on their bridals and black raven-feathered wings on their backs. She smiled at Oceanna and reined in the ponies as she positioned herself for the shot. She drew in the reins, held both in one hand and waved directly at the camera for her cover shot with the other.

The ponies were restless but obedient. The Princess had been training them to pull the chariot for the Fourth of July Festival in Chardon, all during her high school sophomore year, and they knew how to behave in a crowd.

Proudly, confidently, she snapped the reins along their rumps. They sprang into action, rearing up and shaking their long black manes dramatically. Snap, wind, snap. Oceanna got the action shot. Several of Her Highness's girlfriends, still dressed in their cheerleading outfits after marching and demonstrating their moves, leaped onto the back of the Pumpkin Chariot, begging for a ride through the haunted woods, daring the Princess to scare them with a wild ride.

With a spark in her eye, she smiled at her friends, glanced at Oceanna, shrugged, and snapped the reins again. In a spasm, they lurched into a forward gallop down the rolling meadow onto the path through the woods. Her team was wide-eyed and frisky, bumping the chariot along enough to make them scream. Snap. Wind, Snap. Oceanna got it all.

Wooden targets dotted the open field for the axe-throwing contest. Large round bull's-eye targets of red and black concentric circles braced on tripods built of two-by-fours, decorated with tiki torches and jack-o'-lanterns, were set up to receive hurled axes and arrows. The targets stood ready for marksmen to demonstrate their skills, proving who was the best among them. Lifelong hunters lined up, bragging they were sure to win the prizes. More than just trophies, among the rewards, were elegant new hunting compound bows, arrows, longbows, shotguns, and gleaming dressing knives to butcher the catch. All are on display as inspiration. Bonfires were lit at the edges of the shooting range, sparking and spitting. Observers gathered around behind the participants, clapping when their favorite challengers stepped up.

Oceanna worked to get the moments on film, loading and unloading film from the camera back, making sure she had the film fully wound back, and returning the exposed roll to the metal canister before opening and installing the fresh magic plastic. She fumbled in the dark fitting the winding gear cogs in the film's holes just right for a smooth wind from frame to frame. Dad never transitioned to auto-wind models. He had stuck with what had made him successful.

The muscular axe throwers stepped up one by one. They confidently wield their heavy blades, feeling the balance, then hurling them, end over end, at the targets with two hands, expressions serious and focused. Calloused palms and fingers, sensitive to the weight of the wooden handles to the hammer, raising them over their heads, thrusting, calculating the right spin to stick, skillfully thudding the blades deep into the bullseye at thirty paces. Encouraging family and friends oohed and clapped.

Out of the corner of her eye, Oceanna spied movement, a flash of a small head light bobbing through the haunted woods, jiggling along to the tune of a puffing four-stroke engine. She watched the rider straddling the four-wheeler follow the bridal path through the darkening woods as the setting sun blazed crimson clouds in the cobalt sky. The headlight's approach went unnoticed by the large groups of spectators, but Oceanna felt a dangerous chill on its approach.

The rider came closer, passing by the flickering torches. Thick-bodied and strong, it traversed the event, sporting a tall cowboy hat and an overly large Carhartt coat with a rifle across the handlebars and a holster with a pistol on each hip. She rolled up to the competition grass slowly. Oceanna stood still, and the rider puttered up alongside her with a tense smile.

Gretchen stared unblinking at Oceanna, greeting her with a nod. She looked over Oceanna's costume with steely eyes that seemed to scour while Oceanna checked out Gretchen's outfit in return. Ironically, they had both dressed in their father's clothes and carried their father's tools to a festival celebrating transition, the passing from the harvest of fall to the finality of winter.

Gretchen's round eyes shimmered intensely from under the brim of her father's Stetson, big enough to fall over her fluffy bronze eyebrows before settling down on the tops of her ears. Her pale, round, baby doll cheeks contrasted eerily with her dark five-o'clock shadow that bristled from one small ear to the other. Her beard was growing out more than usual. A shift from her self-conscious compulsive shaving. Her hands rested on the long gun lodged on the rifle stalk across the handlebars, as many hunters did in deer season. Her knuckles were red from exposure as she knocked among the brush, riding through the woods.

"Are you in the contest tonight?" Oceanna asked nervously, fondling the camera in her hands. "Can I get a picture of you competing? You're one of the only women… carrying a weapon," she choked and lifted the camera slowly, sensing an aggressive mood, hoping not to trigger any revengeful reactions.

Looking through the lens at Gretchen, she zoomed back to capture her from hat to boot—a heroic figure exuding strength, straddling the rider authoritatively. The women stood together, looking into each other, measuring each other up. Experiencing each other as complex creatures. Oceanna took a picture of a determined survivor. Gretchen's x-ray vision scanned Oceanna for a soul, finding a relentless, bliss-following adventurer. They shared a common spark of independence and the stamp of victory. Twitching muscles transformed Gretchen's plump cheeks into a grizzly frown. Oceanna backed away.

Revving the throttle and shifting into second gear, Gretchen rolled along the edges of the target range, yellow light illuminating her as she trundled in and out of shadows and by the torches along the dark boundaries of the festival. Slowly, she bumped along the grassy perimeter, eyeing the targets. She felt a touch of glee, seeing the torch flames laugh out loud at the pumpkins with wide yaws, jagged teeth, and sneers, mocking them by sticking out her tongue.

The competing archers stepped up and were practicing before the competition began. Archers looked over their longbows and discussed the details of the effects of the tail feathers on distance and direction. At the far edge of the target grounds, the battle reenactment camp was setting off small cannons in salutes to their fallen ancestors. Gretchen felt the storm of envy fill her.

"Why no one loves me? Only my dolls cheering for Gretchen?" Gretchen thought as she watched families gather and pat each other on the back. They called out the names of their champions as each contestant stepped up, "No friends!" she growled low.

Pulling a pistol from its holster with her right hand while holding the throttle down and steering with the right, aiming effortlessly, she blasted the pumpkin-headed infantry soldier, riding a plastic, bones-only steed to bits at ten miles per hour. Reducing the thick-skinned gourd to shreds jerked her into glee. Pieces of the soldier's gray uniform scattered over the tree branches twenty feet above. She roared with laughter and took several more shots. Only Oceanna sensed the gloom in the joke. No one else turned their heads.

Oceanna trotted across the field behind Gretchen as she turned the handlebars back in the direction of the wandering crowds and moved directly at the show on the gazebo, where Dotty Pax and the Pumpkineers were coming back from a break.

Dotty and the band had been playing together for twenty years. When, on the year, they reached the brink of stardom with a hungry record company in Hollywood calling them down to Los Angeles to discuss a possible record deal, they imploded. Elated at the thought of really making it, the band members celebrated their big chance by going out into the thick, hot Hollywood night. They naively purchased a tourist map directing visitors to movie star houses, celebrity restaurants, and the Hollywood Walk of Stars, including the music club hot spots on Sunset Boulevard. They tumbled into the Whisky a Go Go on a night when the featured band was blasting it. The music was great, and the drinks flowed down their necks quickly and in large numbers.

Tragically, after several rounds of free drinks, the lead guitarist, drummer, and a rubbery, passed-out, much younger Dotty Pax crawled into the new Mercedes rented by the studio. They sped down the Sunset Strip, pulsing neon signs and marques flashing rainbow colors reflected off the polished chrome, dazzling the distracted, misty-eyed driver. Unfamiliar with the array of freeway onramps and exits, he turned onto the Hollywood Freeway, going the wrong way, and jammed the pedal down. It was late at night, so the traffic was relatively light, giving time for the drummer, who was driving, to get up to ninety miles per hour before they met the front bumper of the long-haul semi going sixty-right at them.

The impact had been so great that the roof of the Mercedes sheared off at shoulder level, taking the heads off the necks of the drummer and the guitarist in the front passenger seat as smoothly as a new razor-shaving stubble. Dotty Pax, blacked out, laying down in the back seat, came back to consciousness, staring back at two severed heads lying next to her on the blood-soaked rear seat while the jaws of life peeled back the mangled metal to free her. After three weeks in the hospital, she walked out with only deep facial bruises and a load of guilt, and she descended into a depression that she would never be free of.

The remains of the band – Dotty, the violinist, and the bass guitarist – were reduced to entertaining in small, low-pressure venues throughout New York, Cleveland, Chardon, and biker bars in Ashtabula. It wasn't that their playing had become mediocre that erased them from the up-and-coming list. It was that the thrill of stardom had been killed along with their friends.

Dotty's voice had gained depth and intensity, though. It was known that she could break your heart singing the blues. The truth was, she could not help it. Her fans said her version of "At Last" could split a cynic after half a stanza.

At sixty-one years old, Dotty was still a temptress in her tight black witch's dress, her long silver-gray hair hanging down to her waist, deep red nails, and matching lips. She managed to keep her figure by smoking cherry cigars and drinking scotch every day. Life with the band was still an emotional anchor, and it helped with the bills. She sipped her scotch and chatted with the fiddle player about the richness of the yellow full moon that was appearing in the east as the sky glowed with the last rays in the west. Fiddler nodded and drew her slender bow across the strings. Dotty announced, "At Last."

Holding the microphone to her lips, looking out over the easy grounds, the memories returned. Facing agony never got old. It was always agony. She felt it as she sang it. Her heart aching, she let her hurt roll through her gut and ring out through her throat. Tears bubbled, rolling down her gaunt cheeks, streaking trails of mascara, like every time she sang it.

Movement in the distance caught her eye. Something menacing was coming her way. What looked like a cowboy on a trail rider was approaching directly at her across the fields of mowed grass in the dark. Its body language is aggressive and full of intent. Dotty sensed a seething spirit even at that distance.

To avoid disaster, get help, and not cause a panic, she glanced over at the oldest building in the town square to see if she could get the sheriff's attention. He had been watching her from afar all evening while monitoring the visitors at the hall, but he was not looking at her at this moment and missed her glance.

He normally could not take his eyes off her, but tonight, he was showing off the restored brown brick city hall with the date of the township's inception, 1799, in brass numbers over the main entrance. He had his back turned to her, pointing out the steeply pitched, newly shingled roof and cupola, topped by a large copper weathervane in the shape of a strutting rooster, one stiff leg and claw sticking out, crowing. He had a booth with historical pictures of the area, starting from the original hall building and continuing through the restoration last spring. Trick-or-treaters milled around him asking for candy, questioning the sheriff about his dog, eating cotton candy, and standing impatiently in line for the Haunted Hayride wagon to come around to pick them up.

She noticed the cowboy had a rifle across the handlebars and pistols on both hips. Dotty gathered herself, drained the glass of scotch with a jerk, leaned into the microphone, and began the song. Giving it all her power, sending it right to the heart of the cowboy. She could see the desperation in the baby-faced, shiny-eyed creature that fixed on her from under the tattered brim of the old hat. She could see the strain of madness. She knew the look of crazy well because that tortured spirit stared back at her every day from her own mirror since the accident. The night, her world shifted from delighted to devastated. The strange, thick cowboy had the familiar look of a twisted soul.

Oceanna trotted up behind Gretchen, who halted just before the path in front of the stage, remaining in the shadows. She lifted the rifle from her handlebars, pointing the barrel at the ground, the motor idling. Oceanna lifted the camera simultaneously, in what seemed like slow motion, synchronized, moving with the action.

Gretchen felt the cold metal in her fists, stood up on the foot pegs, and swung the rifle up, horizontal, aiming along the heads of the crowd dancing at the foot of the gazebo. Hesitated, then swung up at Dotty when she jerked down the glass of scotch, turning to face the microphone standing mid-stage and hesitated. They faced each other for a moment, held each other's attention, and joined in spirit. Then, Gretchen cocked the gun, pulling back the lever, setting a shell in front of the hammer, ready to fire.

Dotty gripped the microphone with fingertips, pulled her mouth close, and centered herself. The notes threaded through her center, vibrated in every chakra, penetrating her heart at the core, and radiated out her lips, transmitting her dark empathy.

In a second, Gretchen's safe isolation unfolded, loosened. She greeted the shift with suspicion and confusion.

She remembered being invaded and tricked by love before. For a second, she felt a lift. She stood stunned, disoriented on the pegs of her rider, looking around the festival like a sleepwalker coming to. An impossible stirring in her rage-encrusted heart halted her. Her raw spirit had not been shared in so long. Her mind had been blocked for years against connection or hope. A deeper feeling than rage pulled her in, holding her still. She stared at Dotty, alive and pulsing with rhythm under the moon.

Laying out her soul through song had become a necessity for Dotty. It was how she purged hopelessness from her life. Sometimes, the happy side effect of exposing her deep longing was the quickening of a magical muscle that reached in and pried off tight emotional lids for others who suffered, living separately and clamped down.

This time, it was Gretchen's turn. Dotty closed her eyes, combed through her own journey, summoned her magic, and reached out, connecting to Gretchen for that moment to let her know someone understood and that she was not alone. Gretchen's psychic blinders were yanked off. She experienced an overwhelming sensation, much like falling in love, and recoiled.

Shocked and emotionally disarmed, Gretchen gritted her teeth, pulled the gun to her shoulder, swung the barrel up at Dotty, then snapped it high in the direction of the Huntsburg Township Hall's polished copper cock weathervane. Fired once, ejected the shell-like lightning, putting another shell in the barrel and fired it as well, lowered the gun to its comfortable seat on the handlebar stalk from whence it came and rode off, changed and shaky, down the trail, disappearing into the woods on her ride home.

Struggling to stand after dropping to her knees, Oceanna thumbed the winding lever to the thirty-fifth frame, the last shot on the last roll. She looked through the zoom lens, adjusted focus, followed the line of the windows up the roof to the top, framing the cupola, zoomed in tight on the weathervane, and took a picture of the two bullet holes freshly administered by a crack shot. One through the strutting cock's head and one through its heart. Snap.

Dotty's voice never wavered, and the Pumpkineers never missed a note.

17

Control

Nurse Woods shaved everywhere. Rose had never even shaved under her arms. She never had much body hair, being so fair-skinned, but there was thick hair curling in the region of the operation, so a very patient nurse came in and shaved the area, leaving the razor in case Rose wanted to do her legs. Observing the tension in her patient, Woods listened to Rose's list of fears and nodded in the right places. Rose tried to joke about it, but her stomach knotted up at the thought of being laid open, vulnerable, with no one there, just in case. Family approval had been forsaken in high school long ago.

Her mortality staring her in the face, she agonized, waiting on the gurney, watching the IV drip through clear tubes into her arm. She prayed mightily that Oceanna could be by her side. The comfort of feeling a friend standing by her would sustain her. As a last effort to calm herself, she called Oceanna's cell phone to let her know. She tried to hide the panic in her voice while envisioning a knife going into her. She tried to say something funny but failed. Her thoughts trained on defeating a monster that blackened her guts.

She cried her prayers silently, begging to be forgiven for the wrongs she had done. Especially the one for which she figured she was being punished now: the nightmarish abortion she had during her sophomore year in high school. She had shared the ghastly experience with Oceanna over happy-hour apple martinis one night, describing the entire miserable thing, including her well-meaning but unforgiving family, fire-and-brimstone preacher, and protesters outside the clinic, yelling and waving signs with pictures of aborted fetuses. The plague of bullhorns condemned her to hell. Her once-loving father, turning from adoring to ashamed at the news of his little princess participating in sex with a black man she hardly knew, was torture enough, but learning she was with child broke him.

Her parents spent weeks in hard prayer. Initially mustering their faith, when this failed to bring relief, they devolved into harsh judgments, emotional abuse, and confusion. Father endlessly prayed for his little girl, whom he was forced to admit had been lustful and sloppy. She had sinned twice: first, becoming pregnant and then committing the sin of murdering the fetus through abortion. His worst nightmares had come true. He shunned her. The entire family closed off. Her best friend was also far away now. Was that her fault, too?

"How unworthy am I?" she asked herself.

This torture had to be her punishment. Didn't it? An old conversation came to mind. Comments Oceanna had made, almost as an aside, rolled around in her mind. A pagan comment she had made during a discussion they were having about who was going to heaven, if there was one, and who would be left behind.

Rose emptied her first cocktail in a long, deep swallow. "If the rapture comes and you haven't accepted Christ, that's it," Rose explained. "That's the key. I worry about you because you don't believe in the savior. I worry that you will be left behind and go to hell, and I'll miss you."

She twirled the stem of the martini glass between her fingers and looked across the candles on the table at Oceanna sadly.

"Rose, seriously? This idea makes no sense. You're saying that if I murdered my mother and repented, turned the corner, and accepted Christ as the son of God, I'd get a pass? I'd be allowed into heaven before any of the non-Christians? But people who do good in the world get left out?" She winced and narrowed her eyes at Rose. "Like the dedicated monks and nature-loving Native Americans? Tibetan priests? The Jews? All the people who pray and honor some god all day? Prayer is their life!" Oceanna tried to keep her voice soft.

"Other religions don't worship the true ascended son of God. That's the proof! That is the core! None of the other prophets ascended," Rose pressed.

Oceanna smiled and drank down the rest of her green martini.

"I'm totally serious, friend." Rose looked glum.

"I have to keep things simple. This is what I figure it is, Rose. In heaven, there must be perfect justice, right?" She sipped her drink from the wide glass. "No matter what! No matter what else heaven is made of or what amenities it has to be golden streets. Whatever, it will have to have perfect justice, right? Heaven is founded on pristine, perfect justice, right? The one thing everybody seems to trust about God is the delivery of absolutely perfect judgment on who is right and who is wrong... right?" She finished the dregs of her martini. "Heaven is God's flawless justice, rewards for good. To put a fine point on it, no mistakes exist in heaven. Correct?" Oceanna gestured with her finger on the table, pointing around the happy hour side dishes and fried zucchini as she spoke.

Rose leaned back and thought about it. Yes, justice would have to be perfect in God's heaven. She followed the logic and nodded slowly, careful not to get caught in a corner she could not talk her way out of. She nodded.

"So, does it make sense to you that millions of spirits, passionately devoting themselves to prayer and meditation, should go to hell? That's their crime? Not Christian?" Oceanna tipped her head and lowered her voice to a loving tone. "They pray to a different god. The natives should go to hell. Women, because they love women, should drop into hell. That's the same dirty tricks, crappy justice we have down here!" Oceanna leaned back and looked around the bar. "I don't see any justice in that, Rose. Do you?" She slid out of the booth and started to go for another round. The bartender stirred the ice deep in the ice chest with a scraping sound and looked bored.

"If that is perfect justice, fuck it, Rose. I can never believe in that... ascension or no ascension."

She reached for Rose's glass. Taking a long look at her, leaning against the corner of the booth with her windblown, disheveled ponytail curling wildly, blushed cheeks tracing the rim of her glass, she softened. "Not to worry. If anybody deserves a place in heaven, Rose, it's you."

Returning to the present, Rose shook her head, braced herself, and dialed Oceanna, leaving a voicemail telling her she was going under the knife, then hung up. Oceanna would know the terror that meant to Rose. Voices in the hall were getting closer. Sweat trickled down her ribs. She shivered, feeling chilled, stiff, and guilty. It was all she could do not to tear off the needles and run naked down the halls. She prayed some more. "Forgive me, God, forgive me."

Nurse Woods came into the room, fiddled with the knobs on the IV machine, looked at the monitors, and smiled at Rose, who continued to pray, hoping Oceanna would get the message soon and pray for her in her own way—meditating, burning incense and candles, celebrating life by eating big, fat strawberries and sipping champagne hissing in black bottles. It brought a moment of warmth, recalling the evenings they had shared relaxing at her house after a work week of agency drama.

The doctor entered the room and leaned over her, his face covered in a green surgical mask, and instructed her to count down, backward from ten to one. The bright lights and clanking of metal trays and surgical instruments banged her ears, filling her with dread.

"Run, Rose, run!" she thought, clinging to the bed rails, her lips counted, "Ten, nine…"

18

Enter the cardboard landscape

s the sedative flooded in, Rose drifted into a dream, enfolding her, floating her into a cardboard landscape. *The paper doll inhabitants sprung from the crayon drawings of her workshop clients. Driving a red toy convertible car, she steered through a paper doll, pop-up, and storybook world. She grinned and waved back at scribbled, cardboard people cutouts inhabiting fold-out houses and tissue streets under a finger-painted purple sky looming with black cotton ball clouds, foil lightning bolts flashing among them.*

In the tiny back seat, an entire picnic basket sat, filled with food, ready for the party. The seat was piled high with a red-hot, flaming barbecue grill, a cooler full of hot dogs the size of footballs, gallons of pop, several bags of charcoal, cans of lighter fluid, long sharp forks for skewering the hot dogs, and a five-gallon-sized jar of sweet pickle relish for her dear Vernon, who sometimes devoured entire jars of the sweet greens if allowed.

A wave of anxiety crawled over her. She checked her watch, which was shaped like a medicine cabinet. It read two syringes past a blood bag, and she realized she was late for the A.A.S. company picnic.

Tossing on rose-colored sunglasses, she jammed her bare foot down on the gas pedal, igniting the car's thrusters, and squealed down the paper road, leaving smoldering scorch marks. Stress curdled her stomach. She worried about meeting Ken Musk at the party. If she talked to him, he would make lewd suggestions. If she ignored him, he would make grunting noises and accuse her of faking her disgust because she really wanted to take him into her mouth. Intense nausea came over her.

She feared there was no way out and tried to face it.

"Maybe there is no escape. I should just die and get it over with," she mumbled.

Closing her fingers around the skull-and-crossbones steering wheel, she prayed for a guiding light. When, in her peripheral vision, a stretched limo—hot pink and glistening—overtook her and floated up alongside her. The hood was twenty feet long and studded with diamonds. Giant gems glimmered around the hubcaps, flashing so brightly that her retinas ached.

The tinted window rolled down, and there was pathetic Tammy, Ken's work wife, carved of wood, strung with ropes, grinning a wooden scowl. Ken's dutiful secretary belted stiffly to the driver's seat, fingers sewn to the fake fur steering wheel. Her head hinged to her bruised neck with bolts. Her jaw screwed shut.

Rose tried to disguise her panic, waving with a casual flip of her wrist. Tammy's head turned mechanically, wobbling on her neck.

"Hey Tammy! Going to the party?" she whined.

The back window of the limo ground slowly down, revealing Ken's bulbous head, swollen several times too large for his body. Winking and leering with his bulging, watery eyes, he flirted. Lolling up from the back seat behind Tammy, he pulled the ropes that operated her enslaved hands while growling vulgar comments at the back of her head, drooling from a mouth full of knives.

Fisting the ropes screwed to Tammy's wrists, he yanked too hard, intentionally, jerking with such madness that her head almost separated, flopping to the sudden lurches, right and left. His feet kicked the back of Tammy's seat, and he was dressed in thigh-high black boots that buckled up to gynecological exam stirrups on the back of Tammy's headrest. He spurs her ears.

Rose smashed her bare foot on the gas pedal in an attempt to lose them, propelling herself forward, flying over tight curves and rolling hills, burning the paper road, and igniting the tissue-paper bushes, but the limo remained close.

Ken moaned as he turned a crank that lifted a complicated machine gun. He swung it out the window, aiming at Rose, and cocked it. Ken's mouth hung open obscenely and stunk as he panted. He blasted her. Shots rang out, riddling the race car's red, super-glossy paint with bullet holes in one side and out the other. Rose wrestled the stick shift into high gear with a long, wobbly shifter, crashed up the curb onto the sidewalk, and raced Pall Mall through the town.

Ken grimaced, straining the ropes harder. Tammy's wooden legs twisted, responding to his commands, sticking the accelerator, rushing the limo down the street in hot pursuit, sparks crackling from every bearing.

Rose collided with paper houses, flattening them, tore through plastic gardens, over fragile porches held up with popsicle sticks, and flew right over the picnic tables where A.A.S. clients were setting up the cookout party.

She whizzed through the air past Vernon, who whooped and waved a giant spoon, hoping for a jar of relish. He rolled his eyes defiantly and spat at Ken when he zoomed overhead. Ken fired at Vernon, missing him but laying down a spray of bullets so tightly that he cut the picnic table in half and so fast that the lids on a row of relish jars spun open.

Faint and blurry-eyed, Rose felt weak. Her feet were getting wet— it was blood. She had been shot. A fountain of blood was filling the car, bubbling from holes in her belly. She spotted several tall arches not far ahead. She thought there might be a path made of clouds leading to heaven. But as she zoomed closer, the mist evaporated, revealing the graceful braces for the steep onramp to her favorite bridge stretching over Portland's Willamette River. She steered up the ramp. As she ascended, the sky darkened into a black velvet evening. The full moon appeared honey-yellow, with stars twinkling all around.

Anxiety eased. She glided into euphoria. Her lungs filled with fresh air, crisp and cold. She inhaled deeply, wondering how she could feel so free at a time like this.

The city lights sparkled in the landscape below. Perplexed, she wondered if she was entering heaven at last—perhaps her prayers were being answered. But, she wondered, was it appropriate to pass into heaven while being pursued by the devil? Maybe she was not passing into heaven at all.

Ken's rolling thunder pulled up inches from Rose's door, positioning her directly in line with the smoking gun. Rose worked her steering wheel, turning fast and losing control, and spun the race car end over end down the lane like a pinwheel, colliding with the snorting limo and knocking Tammy's head off. Her headless hands remained frozen to the wheel.

Ken, ignoring her uncapped shoulders, rankled the ropes, directing the pink behemoth. The puppet master flailed for control, his heels digging into Tammy's open neck, hands blistering under pressure. The little racer deformed as the diamond bumper flattened it, bringing them both to a steamy halt, squeezing them into a single pile of junk.

Rose hauled open the door, freeing a thick cascade of blood that oozed onto the road. Ken dug himself out of the wreckage and grabbed hold of her collar. Rose pulled away and leaned back over the seat, trying to break Ken's hold. Feeling for a weapon, she grabbed a can of lighter fluid, leaking from the picnic basket and crammed it into Ken's teeth. She drew out a giant, red-tipped stick match as long as a broom handle, scraped it down his bulging pants zipper, and stuck the flame to his face, watching him explode.

Beady-eyed and sizzling, Ken raged on. Maintaining a death grip on Rose's collar, he pulled her to the ground, blood-soaked and wriggling, dragging her to the drop-off edge of the bridge. The torn guardrail sprang wide, exposing the long drop to the river rushing a thousand feet below.

Rose banged him with fists, but he fumed and billowed black smoke, dragging her closer to the brink. Kicking and pounding, Rose could not break free. Even though Ken's hands were burned and blackened, the meat cooked, and his hold was tight.

Kneeling on the edge of the broken street, they hesitated. Motionless and silent, but for the hiss of fat on fire, for a final moment, they looked at each other. Rose stared at the grisly sight of Ken's face turning into charcoal, watching his thin hair turn to crinkly ashes. She felt sorry for him. She gazed at the cold black sky, full of heavenly bodies, then down at the shimmering waters. Her leaking torso hung perilously over the edge, unable to escape. She resigned herself, let go of the fight, and figured she was done.

Three deafening explosions rang out, blasts of a pistol firing. Ken's smoldering body shook and shocked, shivered, and splattered as he leaned over Rose's face. His enormous skull erupted. The meatless bones of his hands fell apart, releasing Rose as her collar disintegrated in his grip. His blackened bits tumbled over the edge and down the long fall into the waters below with a hiss.

Groggy and confused, Rose opened sticky eyes and tried to orient herself. She realized she was at the hospital and wanted to know if she was clear of cancer. An unmasked Nurse Woods stepped over to her and smiled.

"You made it, Rose!" Woods checked her pulse at her wrist with warm fingers.

"Did you get it all?" Her lips stuck together and felt papery.

"Your prognosis is good, young lady. The doctor will be around to confirm, but he was very pleased with the results when I talked to him a moment ago. Congratulations!"

Rose closed her eyes and thanked God, hoping it was not a premature congratulations, and started to cry.

The phone rang, but she couldn't move well or climb over the bed rails in time to answer it. She knew it was Oceanna on cue. She couldn't wait to tell her that she had had a nightmare that was going to function well in the final chapter of her mystery novel.

19

D.V.M. Uhglee

Gretchen covered her ears and coiled herself up as small as she could in the corner of the closet. A healthy diesel engine growled and idled at the bottom of the steps while the driver knocked robustly, attempting to rouse someone who could direct him to his rightful destination. The vials of horse vaccinations were safe in the cooler for now, but the sun was getting higher, and the temperature was rising. He needed to deliver this stuff soon or risk losing his laid-back delivery job and the fun of driving a flashy, jacked-up truck all around the countryside. He continued to pound the thick door.

Gretchen cowered. She had glimpsed the sign on the passenger door of the truck displaying the company's initials, D.V.M., over a large gold five-pointed star with the jaunty company motto below, reading, "Veterinary Medicines Delivered at a Gallop."

In frustration, he wiped the sweat from his brow with a pass over the crook of his arm, turned around, jogged down the steps, pulled himself up into the black leather driver's seat, tapped the G.P.S. screen on the dash, checked the address, found his error, and pulled away. Trundling down the long dirt driveway, dust rolling up, back to the buggy path, he was back on course. He pulled away with a roar.

Gretchen was horrified. Was he back again? The doctor. The torturer. The truck and logo looked similar. She could match the shapes of the letters but had never been able to learn to read whole words. The D.V.M. shapes shocked her. Those shapes hit her like a shovel, smashing her face.

In the past, the D.V.M. sign introduced Doctor Mitt Uhglee, the Doctor of Veterinary Medicine who came in a black truck, knocked hard on the door, and joined Gustoff in his ghastly pleasures. They were a sick team, drinking, laughing, and drooling over what they had done or wanted to do. Keeping each other's secrets, they maintained control over their captives, isolating them and keeping them alive enough.

She had figured out how to survive by herself—how to hide, where to hide, when to crawl away. She avoided getting hit by curling up in the closet and climbing into haystacks, barn lofts, and dark places. Then, feeling guilty and fragile, Mother took the brunt of the beatings. Mother couldn't run, and she had paralyzed legs after losing one intense domestic battle, being beaten and dragged by her long hair up the stairs by her husband. It's just the way he liked it. Broken back, nothing she could do.

During monthly visits, Doctor Uhglee would check her out, seeing to mother's health needs after seeing to the horses, Lake Pearl in particular. Sometimes, he would be invited to watch Gustoff assault his wife. Other times, he would be invited to use her himself, while Gustoff enjoyed the phenomena from across the room. Sometimes, little Gretchen would be pulled out and forced to participate. If, and when any hurts were so deep that there needed to be a stitch or two in the face or fanny, the doctor would be available to patch people up discreetly.

In exchange for his professional courtesy, Gustoff would allow a mare to be inseminated with Lake Pearl's precious semen. As an extension of Gustoff, Lake Pearl was everything the man was not: tall, golden, graceful, sweet-natured, pleasant, and much more humane. It was the only healthy relationship Gustoff was able to maintain.

Recalling her father's brand of "love" caused her to wince. He had explained to her that after mother had passed, she was to be his little wife, including her obedience, participating in all his favorite freakish wifely duties. Gretchen already understood what that meant, until death do us part. In other words, until he would kill her, too.

In her head, that final day started to replay, rolling out like a horror movie behind the lids of her watery eyes. She recalled the atmosphere in the barn, misty and gray. Hay bales emitted fog as they dried, piled five bales high in the middle of the wide barn. She could smell the roses growing outside Lake Pearl's stall and see the sun illuminating the red petals, dew catching the sun, sparkling. She felt the warmth of the day just starting, felt her feet in her slippers as she skipped along the barn's dirt floor. She smelled horses and hay, the green and yellow tractor's grease, and admired its ready strength and thick black tires.

Her mouth drew up in a slight smile when she recalled the kittens mewing in their straw nest with the mother cat curled around them, safe and warm. The smell of guns stored in their racks, cleaned, oiled, and loaded by her own hands, just as her father had taught her, stirred her grim thoughts.

She recalled how sore her body was from performing as her father's "wife" the night before. Flinching and rubbing her neck when thinking of his vice-like grip around her throat. She rolled into a tighter ball. Recalling the stabbing pain between her thighs as he raped her caused her heart to pound.

That day felt different somehow. Her emotions were rawer than usual, her agitation more intense. She remembered feeling more on edge, angrier than she was on most mornings. Tired of feeling sore and used, after five years of being his little wife, her patience had eroded. She struggled not to show it; the beatings got worse when she fought back or cried. In desperation, she had developed a mystical habit of leaving her body. She had adapted, learning to lift herself in spirit out of harm's way, leaving behind the body that could not follow. Leaping out like a puff of smoke, she would float at the ceiling, watching as she was brutalized.

"Aware but not there." She rocked and chanted to her pockets stuffed with rag doll miniatures, who listened intently.

The dolls joined the chant. "Aware but not there. Aware but not there."

Remembering that final day, she tried to unravel the changes that had freed her rage. It had been so many years ago. The images flickered torturously, playing in slow sequence, drawing her in. Engrossed in her nightmare, fretting as if it were happening again, she suffered.

On that ancient, fateful day, Gustoff rode up that morning so straight and proud astride Lake Pearl, trotting effortlessly. Four white stockings glided smoothly over the grass while his pale mane and tail fluttered. His yellow-gold coat glistened over rippling young muscles. He puffed his pink nostrils in and out as he entered the barn, sniffing for the grain he anticipated with vigor. He seemed to smile at Gretchen as he trotted past her, grateful that she had mucked out his stall, freshened the water, and delivered his sweet oats.

Lake Pearl was innocent, lovely, and the apple of her father's eye. He was adored by her father and admired by all the owners who brought their mares to breed. She envied him. Lake Pearl was precious.

That day, the lack of respect gnawed at her gut and twisted her mind. The shame her father had deliberately fostered in his child began to take a fatally dangerous turn.

Just a few miles away, at the same time, Oceanna and Dad slowly made their way through the parking lot of Mary Mullet's Breakfast Café, navigating among the black buggies, horses, and construction trucks. It was one of those practical spots that was always crowded; the food was heaped on the plates and undeniably good. The hand-carved sign in the big window announced their hours: open from 5 a.m. to 2 p.m., Monday through Saturday, never on the Sabbath.

The Amish-owned eatery had rows of buggy shelters along the edge of the parking lot, complete with hitching posts and water buckets for up to fifteen buggies at a time. Mary's brother had built the thick wooden booths that accommodated large parties of workmen in heavy work boots and suspenders, seating eight to a booth. Handcrafted iron hooks lined the entry hall, fastened securely to beams with bolts, ready to hold thick winter gear and the obligatory straw hats of the Amish men.

By the time Dad managed to steady his walker and crunch across the rutted parking lot—grooved deeply by thin buggy wheels and horseshoes after the rains had softened the ground—the last table had already been taken. They were preparing to wait when Dad's contractor, Mr. Burkholder, waved them over to join him at his smaller table. He was just placing his order and wanted to ask how the metal roof was working out.

Burkholder's toothy smile revealed an even row of white squares above his shaggy beard. His active curiosity and boundless patience made him a favorite conversationalist, though not always approved of by the bishop. His family had settled in Montville in the 1700s, growing corn and raising horses on the same two hundred acres for two hundred years. He was either related to or had firsthand knowledge of every family in the area, all local events, and even bits of intriguing town history. Known for his gossiping tendencies, he loved to chat.

He shook Oceanna's hand with a powerful grip, his palms the size and texture of a well-oiled baseball mitt. Then he happily assisted Dad into his chair, folded the metal walker to keep it out of the waitress's way, and flagged her down to take their orders.

Dad and Oceanna ordered their usual: eggs over easy with four strips of thick pepper bacon, hash browns, and coffee. Burkholder opted for the massive Workman's Meal, which included six eggs, four strips of bacon, four-link sausages, pancakes, piles of hash browns, flaky, secret-recipe biscuits with fresh, hand-churned butter, and homemade grape jam. All the ingredients came fresh from farms within a mile or two of Mullet's.

After discussing the details of the black metal roof with leafless gutters and the septic tank—and confirming everything was working well, Oceanna decided to ask about Montville lore involving Gretchen Loves, her family, and Gustloff's murder.

"What do you know about the Loves, John?" she asked. "When we go to her home to check on her, there's this feeling of something looming or hovering. It gives me the chills. Like a spirit haunting?" She shrugged her shoulders.

Burkholder looked down at his eggs, tucked his shaggy beard into his shirt to keep it out of the yolks, and continued chewing.

"You probably saw her now and then; she lives pretty close," Dad commented, glancing up at Burkholder's blushing cheeks. He tore a hot biscuit in half and slathered on the soft butter.

Oceanna tucked her napkin into her collar, sensing Burkholder's unease but continuing to pose questions in a gentler tone. His antique family farm shared a patch of road along a stretch of backroad buggy trail at the furthest edge of his acreage.

"Did you ever see her—Gretchen or the mom?" Oceanna leaned in to hear him over the loud laughter and clatter from the kitchen. Dad casually sipped his steaming coffee, watching silently.

"That's an old story." He nodded, looking up from his plate directly into Oceanna's face, a curious light in his eye. He set down his fork. "The story goes that the father, Gustoff, was mean—more than mean. He talked to the men around here normally enough, bragging about his prize stallion. Lots of farmers wanted to go with Lake Pearl because it had a gentle and smart nature. His offspring were like that too, perfect for safely carrying families down the highways."

He cut up his sausages with the butter knife. "The women . . . thought he was strange." He winked at Dad. "They believed the talk that he hit his wife. She fell down their big staircase or something, broke her back, and never came out again!" He stuffed several slices of bacon into his mouth and sipped his coffee. "The rumor was that he broke her back on purpose."

He felt his excitement leaking into his words and made an effort to swallow them along with his sausage. Noticing Dad missing his coffee cup with the cream, he reached over to steady him.

"Did you know him, John?" Oceanna asked.

The sandy texture of his fingers tickled the back of Dad's thin skin as they stirred the cream together. For a second, it seemed he was tearing up.

"Yeah. I knew him and his girl. I knew Gretchen as a little girl, watching us boys train ponies on his hack track. It used to be the best in Huntsburg—covered about a hundred acres, beautiful and smooth. Gretchen would sit on the fence and watch us go around and clap for us." The corners of his lips turned up as he nodded, recalling the memory. "She used to hold my hat for me and put it on her head." He sighed. "She was kind of slow. Sweet, but slow. I don't think she ever spent a day in school."

"So, he was brutal?" Dad asked, watching John cut swaths of stacked pancakes into triangle shapes and stuff them into his mouth. His bulging cheeks gave him a moment to rest from the interrogation.

"Yeah. I saw bruises sometimes—on her wrists and neck." He dabbed his mouth with a bunched-up paper napkin and leaned closer, whispering. "That was not from working in the barn."

"The barn has a strange black mud on the ground in that last stall. It sticks to you if you walk in it, and it smells like rot." Oceanna glanced at the cook, who was placing heavy plates filled with food on the serving ledge, ready to be delivered. She recalled the penetrating smell of the mud and felt a little sick. "What happened in the barn? Do you know?"

"Do you think the kid shot him?" Dad blurted out, blowing on his coffee as he watched the changes in Burkholder's expression.

"I can tell you're a newsman, Jack," he said. "I don't think the sheriff ever blamed her, even though she was the only one there. Her mother had been gone for years." A cloud of deep emotion passed over his face, and an uncomfortable feeling of overexposure crept in.

The table fell silent for a moment as the seriousness of the allegation hung over them.

"What was the mother's name? April or August? Something like that," Oceanna said.

"Rumor, too, that he may have killed her?" Dad added.

"Yeah. It was suspicious. She was much younger. Strange that she would fall like that by accident."

Burkholder pulled a pack of filterless cigarettes from his front shirt pocket, extracted one, and tapped it on the table, packing the tobacco in tight. Oceanna felt a craving for nicotine as she watched him.

"I guess Gustoff thought he got away with it," Dad said. "How come nobody did anything if he was doing all this evil stuff? The sheriff had to look into it?" His voice dropped to a quiet, cautious tone. He understood what could happen to whistleblowers and informants. "Who protected him?" His eyes brightened at the possibilities of conspiracy.

Burkholder stuck the cigarette in his mouth, lit it with a worn silver lighter, and leaned back in his chair.

"Gustoff had friends at the sheriff's office. They looked the other way. The sheriff's mounts are mostly Lake Pearl's kin!" Burkholder leaned closer. "We think it was . . . Doctor Uhglee." His voice dropped to a quiet tone as he glanced across the room at the other tables to see who was sitting there.

"Who?" Oceanna whispered, holding a greasy link sausage between her fingers. "The veterinarian? You're kidding."

Dad looked at her, shushed her with buttery lips, and nodded almost imperceptibly.

"He was powerful in the community—delivered calves and foals, gave shots to the livestock. We all depended on him. He came to the house, took care of sick kids, often for free, and checked and vaccinated children. He even delivered babies in a pinch. This is the country. No one wanted to mess with Doctor Uhglee," Burkholder said, staring at the cigarette between his fingers.

She shook her head and grimaced. "That's the monster's real name? Doctor Uhglee?"

The cashier's phone rang, its vibrating bell cutting through the chatter. Mary Mullet answered it herself. A siren wailed from down the street at the firehouse, summoning volunteers. She slammed down the phone and yelled, "All firemen get moving! Fire! Loves' farm is on fire! Pump truck's on its way! Fire!"

In a unified leap, the room jerked into action. The roar of chairs sliding and boots stomping across the wooden floor was thunderous. Every man stood from his table and rushed to the door as a unit. They grabbed their coats and hats, untied the horses, jumped into their buggies, or climbed into the backs of construction trucks and held on.

Burkholder pulled Dad from his seat, clutching him under his arm and carrying him to the door, his old legs dangling. Oceanna grabbed the walker, rushed to the Jeep with its top down, and started it.

Dad was lifted into the front seat and buckled in before Burkholder jumped into the back seat.

"Head to the back trails! I'll show ya! Over there! We can beat them all!" He tossed his hat onto the back seat and clawed at the roll bar.

Jack Pontiac grinned madly, caught up in the rush of the emergency. Held in by the tight seatbelt, he bounced and tossed in his seat as the wind rushed over him. They dashed over hills and dipped low along gullies. Dad's cheeks flushed, his heart pounded, and his eyes widened with thrill. Just like the old days! Fire!

20

Ascension

Plagued by the memory of her revenge, Gretchen held her head in her hands and stared at the floor, haunted by the final humiliation from her father's voice. She recalled the cut of his words, the shame she had endured, and the moment she'd had enough. Her face flushed with anger as her body trembled with rage. With his dreadful words, Gustoff had sealed his fate.

She relived the punishment: "Stupid girl! Gretchen, no boy wants you for his girlfriend! You are fat, that's not their type! They want virgins!"

Gustoff chuckled as he dismounted Lake Pearl, swinging his leg forcefully over the saddle and scraping Gretchen's cheek with his boot heel. She staggered back several steps until her hips collided with the long wooden gun rack. Her heart pounded, and blood trickled from her cheek.

"I tell you the truth because I love you, idiotic bitch." He loosened the saddle straps, gently lifted it from Lake Pearl's back, and placed it on the stall gate. "Amish boys are beaten by their fathers if they go with English girls!" he growled through gritted teeth.

Seizing her shoulder roughly, he shook her so hard her head jerked back and forth, her eyes rattling in their sockets and distorting her vision.

"You smell bad. Boys don't like that. They want fresh, and that's not you." He leaned in, nose to nose, sniffing her and rubbing his face into her neck.

She squeezed her arms tightly to her chest and pushed him away, sniffing her own shirt, wondering if it was true.

"Maybe you have another infection? You better wash hard! The doctor will have to take care of it the next time he comes." He grinned cruelly. She could feel his breath hot against her face.

Returning to reality, she knew where she was. She stood up from the corner where she had hidden from the delivery man and staggered, feeling nauseous. The events of that bloody day continued to play in her mind, moment by awful moment, ticking along in slow motion and giving her no control over the re-experiencing.

The first day she had taken control of her future had redefined her. Straight-backed and resolved, no longer the victim but the victor, she stood. Her feet were numb as she passed through the dark living room, the familiar rough wooden floor scraping against her bare soles. Gripping the cast-iron door handle, she hauled the door open. She stepped down the front porch stairs and along the path to the barn, her father's cruelty burning into her mind.

She recalled that day:

"You are mine, little pig," Gustoff had said. "Your fat face is as ugly as your butt. What happened? You're growing a beard! Look! Feel that!" He stroked her cheek forcefully and slapped her.

She spun around, turning her back to him, fighting hard not to cry. Snatching a two-by-four that braced the rifle stocks, she wheeled around and swung it low, slamming Gustoff in the groin and dropping him to his knees in agony.

"No!" she yelled.

He cussed her in German, coughing and gagging. Crawling nearer to her, he yanked the wood from her hands. Still on his knees, he swung it at her legs with all his might. Missing contact with bone, he hurled the wood wildly, striking the gun rack behind her. The impact dislodged the weapons from their hand-carved braces, scattering them across the worktable and dirt floor.

"I'm gonna really punish you this time! You think you're sore now? Ha! You're really gonna feel it this time! I'm gonna fix you like I fixed your mother; you bitch!" Gustoff worked to stagger to his feet. "I own you, stupid! You're mine! Guess what—after I break your back, I'll burn those ugly dolls you love so much!"

He turned his head up to meet her eyes and spat at her, then suddenly lurched toward her.

"No!" she shrieked, tears breaking free and flooding her cheeks. She felt the restraint within her finally shatter. The fear that had pinned her to his slavery snapped.

Grabbing the first pistol lying near her, the grip felt as natural in her palm as a spoon. Leveling it at her father, she pulled the trigger, striking him on the thigh and dropping him to his knees. Blood gushed from the wound.

She laughed from deep within her gut for the first time in her life and shot again several times. He yanked the saddle from the gate and pulled it over his chest as a shield. Throwing himself backward into Lake Pearl's stall, he pressed against the horse's hot, golden belly and struggled to pull the wooden gate closed. The horse jerked his head from the oats, ears pinned back and eyes wide with alarm.

Her rescue was automatic—self-preservation, lift-off. The separation from her body felt natural and frequent now. She had practiced her escape during confrontations with overwhelming roughness. Initially, she had been surprised by the sensation of exiting her flesh; the softness of the other world had empowered her. Hovering above herself, observing these sadistic situations had become routine.

Lake Pearl, startled in his stall while enjoying his sweet oats, became frantic at the roar of gunfire. Now Gustoff was crowding into his space, pressing against his belly. Confusion and frustration overtook the stallion. He began to kick violently, shattering the stall walls and fracturing wood and bones alike.

She recalled floating close to the horse's ear, like a friendly ghost, trying to whisper reassurances while looking down on her father. He was scrambling on the ground, panicked and spraying blood.

Her mind had flipped beyond the boundaries of logic, consumed by rage, rolling like a river over the edge of a waterfall. The momentum was unstoppable. She vented her pain into Gustoff, fully satisfying herself that his price had been paid. The price for his conceit and greed was death.

She reloaded the pistol, pouring out the spent shells, inserting fresh ones, and firing again into the stall until the chambers became too hot to handle. Then she chose another rifle or pistol, emptying all its rounds as well. Her eyes stayed focused with singular intent. Her movements were efficient and unyielding. Her ears went deaf from the explosions, and the ringing lasted for days afterward, she recalled.

Lake Pearl became a victim as well. His beauty and innocence were ruined by association. He whinnied, kicked, and stamped as the bullets tore into him. Bucking against the stall walls, spinning and trying to climb over the rails, his hooves became slick with Gustoff's guts as well as his own gore. Blood spurted from his neck and chest until he fell to the ground on top of Gustoff's lead-riddled body. He heaved his last breath, crushing whatever life might have been left in either of them.

Gretchen fired every gun and bullet she could until her fingers were too blistered and cramped with exhaustion to pull the trigger. The barrels were red-hot and smoking. Shell casings scattered at her bare feet, leaving red burn marks on her skin and singing her legs as they were dumped out, still glowing.

Today, she found herself standing in the barn, facing the same stall she had faced that day years before. She sniffed the fragrant air, bright with the scents of sun and hay. She inhaled deeply, squinting at the beams of yellow light streaking in through the gaps in the old boards.

She took long looks at the loft where she had once played and hidden when necessary, recalling the safe nests that had soothed her. Finally, she accepted her fate and found herself able to say goodbye.

She felt herself letting go of the old life: the grassy yard, the fat chickens roosting here and there, the kittens playing with each other in the vegetable boxes, their whiskers glistening in the morning sun. The things she had loved had become daily heartbreaks, too difficult to protect. It had all become too much to bear. Keeping deep secrets had taken its toll. The isolation and guilt, over time, had finally crushed her.

Calmly, she cut the bands binding the hay bales and carefully spread the dry grasses along the barn walls, around the stalls, and fluffed it knee-high in Lake Pearl's stall. Her feet stuck to the black dirt, the decaying evidence of her revenge. She tossed in several dry leather saddles and some old rags, drenching them with gasoline. Gallons of lamp oil were poured onto the hay stacked in the middle of the barn. She cut the gas lines of the tractor and her beloved four-wheel rider, letting the fuel drain onto the ground, forming pools beneath them. She prepared to take the past with her.

Pulling the first stick match from the box, she hesitated, taking one last long look at the life she had known. She thought about her mother and felt both proud and anguished. Quietly, she struck a match and set fire to the stall. The oils burst into flame. She struck another match to the gun bench she had carefully maintained for so long. Yellow flames flickered and began consuming the dry wood of the rack itself.

Climbing onto the stack of hay bales in the middle of the barn, she watched as the fire spread up the wooden planks of the walls and toward the roof. Finally, she struck the last match to the hay beneath her.

As soon as her feet caught fire, she lifted out of her flesh, relieved never to have to walk as Gretchen again. She looked back once to confirm that her body would be safely reduced to ash, determined to leave no future on Earth to return to.

She had done the best she could to deliver justice, pushing back against guilt and hopelessness for as long as she could. Now, she freed herself, leaving others to right the wrongs.

No longer able to smell the burning oil and painted wood, she left her body below and floated among the flames, untouched, becoming part of the brightness. She watched the grass turn to ash. Leaving her body, she became one of the ribbons of black smoke curling upward, racing to the roof and carrying hot cinders that slipped through the seams in the wood and twinkled red-hot.

Existing as an essence, she rose up through the shingles into the blue sky, blackened with roiling smoke. She followed the smoke like a bubble filled with breath, lifted by the heat and the draft of the fire. Gretchen spun with the wind, like a cloud, over the very top of the roof.

The grand rearing horse weathervane spun madly. Overheating and softening, the metal began to curl and eventually came apart. She moved among the white-hot fragments, feeling sad that it was ruined but reassured that little evidence would remain to sift through.

A handful of Amish men galloped up on unsaddled horses, loping down the long driveway and leaping over split-rail fences from across the fields. Gretchen watched them dismount and began hand-pumping water from the old well, forming a bucket brigade with seamless teamwork.

Several buggies rattled up the drive, their horses lurching and sweating. The men yelled to one another as they organized the effort to save what they could, their long beards fluttering vertically in the drafts from the intensifying heat. She admired them from above, gliding overhead. Their brown necks strained as they hollered in their special German. She moved closer, looking into their flushed, red faces from just an inch away, unseen and unnoticed.

She understood and embraced her transformation. She was no longer the same. They did not recognize her as a ghost, too preoccupied to notice her soft whispers of thanks as they labored on.

The red Jeep sped up the driveway after them, rattling as Dad and Oceanna were jostled in their seats. Burkholder bounced around the back seat like a pinball, his hands white-knuckling the overhead roll bar to avoid being tossed out. The Jeep roared up as close as they dared to the inferno.

Burkholder clambered over the rear tailgate, ran up the front porch stairs, and disappeared into the house.

Dad unbuckled his seatbelt before the vehicle fully stopped and instructed Oceanna to retrieve the cameras from the chest riveted to the floor. Grabbing his cane, he tumbled over the running boards and onto the grass.

Oceanna unbuckled the metal lids of the chest, checked two cameras for film, tossed their neck straps over her head, and sprinted after her father. He stood dangerously close to the incinerating structure, yelling at her to frame the shot and capture the action, grinning morbidly from ear to ear.

Gretchen watched from on high as the Jeep slid to a halt and was stunned to see Burkholder climbing out and charging toward the house. Her mood escalated to zeal. She moved after him, floating just behind his neck. He stomped up the stone steps, found the front door open, and yelled for everyone to get out. No answer came.

She stayed at his back as he rooted through every room, praying he was looking for her. She had missed him—her only childhood crush and playmate.

He rushed through the house, calling her name, opening cupboards, and pulling back curtains. Clambering up the stairs, he crashed open every door. When he yanked open her closet door, he froze and began to cry.

The sight of her secret nest touched him. He understood her need for a hiding place: blankets folded and fashioned into a crude mattress, blankets rolled up, towels used as pillows, and a family of handmade miniature rag dolls lined along the edges. Each doll was shaped to comfort her, a horse, a cat, chickens, and human figures dressed in Amish children's costumes.

Above the bed, her mother's old coats and dresses hung as buffers against a harsh reality. He understood whom she had been hiding from, alone against the nightmares that surrounded her. Shame for not saving her seared his heart. He snatched the boy doll that resembled him and shoved it into his shirt.

Gretchen hovered near his ruddy, bristled cheek and tried to whisper in his ear that she had loved him. She witnessed tears falling from his blue eyes, felt his sorrow, and became forever altered. She experienced an ultimate epiphany that jolted her, shattering the dim confinement of her shame and transforming her into a gleaming, radiant soul. At that moment, she realized she had been loved.

He reeled about, leaped down the stairs, and ran out into the line of men pouring water on a lost cause. The fire raged, so intense that the water they tossed evaporated instantly. The heat singed their beards, and the barn, now a wall of flame, roared and rushed, sucking the air from their lungs.

Hot ash fell like snow over the house and yard. Horses reared and fled into greener pastures as far as they could go, some dragging buggies along without drivers, heading for home.

Oceanna framed the disaster, following Dad's directions for each master shot perfectly.

"Frame wide! Get the barn, the rearing horses, and the pasture behind!" Jack Pontiac called out, pointing his crooked fingers like he was conducting an orchestra. "Make sure the focus is clear! Don't let the brightness wash out the men's faces! Adjust!"

Ashes fluttered thick in the air, catching in his throat. He spat them out and continued, red-faced and blustering. Jack felt life return to him. He had missed this affirming drama more than he realized. The crush of looming doom invigorated his instincts, and the defiance of death charged him. Survival swirled around, colliding with uncertain existence, irresistible.

Oceanna snapped shots of the flames consuming the barn, billowing black smoke rolling into the fresh blue sky. The fire overtook the thick beams, shattered the glass in the cupola, and exploded stored fuels. Bullets left unspent began to ignite, black powder heating and blasting lead through the walls of fire.

Shrapnel scattered across the yard, hitting willy-nilly. Fragments ricocheted off the Jeep and rattled into Oceanna, scoring her skin. She bled and cussed at Dad but held her position, continuing to capture the tragedy as it worsened with every passing second.

She snapped a picture of her father, filled with enthusiasm, standing in the foreground. He leaned on his cane with one hand and pointed at the fire with the other. Ashes fell onto his stooped shoulders, and cinders lit small fires in his thin gray hair. Grinning like a madman, his eyes shone with glee, while in the background, men bailed water onto a wall of fire teetering on the verge of collapse. Heroism unfolded, frozen in time by her lens. She had to admit, she experienced a wretched kind of bliss.

Gretchen felt her anger evaporate. The burdens she had carried disintegrated like the barn. All that remained was her epiphany of love. Now, she truly was a particle of light—shining, floating upward, gliding on the wind into the deep blue ecstasy.

As she ascended, she looked back once at the chaos she had unleashed. She saw the men fall back, conceding to the finality of the flames. They retreated, calling to one another to tend their blistered hands and let the barn burn itself out.

She watched Jack Pontiac collapse in her little garden, overcome by smoke and heat. When the beams gave way, the walls fell flat, erasing the crimes committed over long years of pain.

Gretchen released her emotional grip, untethering herself from family, community, and Earth. She floated into the sky—a thousand feet high, then a mile, then beyond the clouds and the romantic moon. She became part of the universe, moving toward an unknown destination, taking her bliss with her.

She flew on.

21
At Last!

On the short limo ride to meet Oceanna for their radio interview, Rose leaned back in the plush seat of the black limousine. Striking a match, she touched the flame to the medicine and inhaled deeply. The weed hissed and popped as she drew in, her lips tight around the paper cigarette. The burnt flavor rolled over her tongue, robust and oily. Her lungs felt warm as the blue smoke disintegrated into them, bringing relief from pain and illuminating her mind with the fresh beauties of the world.

She leaned back into the soft leather seat, closed her eyes, and let the infusion take the tension from her sore back and anxious thoughts. She drifted, floating in the long limousine, stretched out, feet up like a queen. The perfectly groomed, very butch-lady driver smiled and rolled open the sunroof with the press of a button to avoid being affected by the dense cloud herself.

Fresh air and bright sunlight swirled in as the smoke rolled out, fading into the summer sky. Rose inhaled the clean air several times, filling her tingling lungs. The sun beamed down, crossing her closed eyelids. Through the fragile skin of her lids, she saw delicate veins, like black spider webs against a yellow curtain. She imagined herself as a translucent rose petal soaking up the rays, becoming invigorated and strong like the sun itself.

A soft hum escaped her lips, blending with the jazz lilting through the well-balanced speakers. The music enfolded her, its vibrations dissolving her spirit into an effortless glide among the notes.

Thoughts of Oceanna gave her chills. The longing to hold her, to surround herself with her presence, had haunted Rose daily. The idea of tasting her had filled her dreams at night. She worried that her obsession was one-sided, fearing a heartbreak so agonizing that she dared not let the thought enter her mind.

Yet, there was no escape. She had to try, forced to accept whatever happened. This would be the first time she truly felt open, desperately hoping the feelings were mutual.

Today was the day her questions would be answered.

Oceanna was waiting for her now. They were scheduled for an interview with a Channel 12 talk show host to discuss the last twenty-four months of their lives, including Oceanna's frantic race from Portland to rescue her father, a journey that led deep into Amish country; Jack Pontiac's Pulitzer Prize and his induction into Washington, D.C.'s Newseum; Rose's battle with cancer, highlighting her struggle to survive; and the pact Rose and Oceanna made to write books together long-distance, an effort to revive their disintegrating hopes and resolve some of their personal struggles along the way.

The news anchor planned to cover the entire saga, including how the painful life of Gretchen Loves and the murder of her father had become a mystery ultimately solved by the Pontiacs. The story culminated in Gretchen's dramatic suicide by fire and Jack Pontiac's collapse at the scene. The events, captured in a series of well-framed black-and-white photos, had ignited interest in Oceanna's book and propelled Rose and Oceanna into the limelight as newsworthy heroes and authors.

Rose was relieved to be high, allowing Oceanna to take the reins. She wanted to cling to her and trusted that the long day of public appearances would eventually end—the interview and dinner done— so the real moments could begin, finally, in private.

Leaning her cheek against the door, Rose watched the tall downtown buildings glide past. The theater's colorful, flashing marquee, bustling pedestrians weaving along their intertwined courses, and street musicians banging drums and guitars filled her vision. Their voices carried the melodies of the streets. Electric trains whispered across intersections, faces in the windows looking out at her limousine, some pointing, hoping to glimpse a star. She giggled at the thought, realizing she sort of was one now.

Traffic was heavy, making the ascent up Broadway to the Benson Hotel both agonizing and thrilling. And there she was, standing on the curb, waiting, dressed to the nines in a silky, well-fitted gray suit. Her arms were full of long-stem roses, a bucket of ice, a bottle of pale champagne, and two crystal flutes dangling delicately from her fingers. Her short blond hair was tied into playful pigtails.

Rose sighed and braced herself, her heart pounding.

Oceanna waited in the grip of anticipation, sweating under her new jacket. After all the jangling events of the last couple of years, this was the moment of real terror. Her question was simple but overwhelming: Could she fit into what Rose wanted her to be? Just a friend, if that was all? Would she push too hard and risk wrecking their relationship?

Spinning in circles of doubt and second-guessing had become tedious and ridiculous. Today, she would get her answer. Whether she liked what Rose wanted or not, the time had come. Did she love her or not? Oceanna would investigate her face and find out.

The long car glided up to the curb in front of her, glistening and purring.

The handsome, uniformed driver stepped out, walked around to the passenger side, smiled at Oceanna knowingly, and pulled open the door. Arms full, Oceanna dropped onto the seat with a clank, drew in her legs, and found herself hip to hip, staring into the face she had imagined since she'd left.

Paler and thinner now, a faint blush bloomed across Rose's cheeks as they looked at each other in wonder.

"Hello," Oceanna said, her eyes locked on Rose's, inches from her face.

"I missed you." Rose started to cry. She looked down at her hands, wringing them. "They took my lady parts," she whispered, her voice filled with shame. Her tearful eyes turned up to Oceanna's, streams running down her cheeks.

"Yes, Rose. I'm sorry," Oceanna said, setting down the bucket and reaching out to touch her hands, giving them a gentle squeeze.

"And… my hair fell out. Look! No eyebrows." Tears trickled down Rose's face as she pulled the scarf from her head. Short blond wisps of hair blew about like feathers—white and baby-fine, like the down of a chick.

"It's all right, Rose." Tears welled up in Oceanna's eyes and spilled down her face. "You're perfect if you didn't know." A timid smile trembled along her lips.

"I need to tell you something." Rose slid her trembling fingers around Oceanna's neck. She felt the silk of her skin, damp with perspiration, and pulled her face close. "I think I . . . have fallen in… love."

Daring to lean in close, Rose needed to cross the old boundary between them. She smelled the warm, rich scent of amber as she brushed her lips across Oceanna's chin and pressed her mouth onto hers. With her eyes open, Rose took Oceanna's tongue into her mouth. Oceanna breathed deeply, relaxed, and let Rose take her time.

The flowers crushed between their breasts, releasing red petals that fell into their laps, carrying their sweet fragrance. Their kisses were deep and slow, Oceanna responding to Rose's offering in kind, stirring each other. They gazed into each other's eyes and smiled, amazed.

Oceanna reached for the ice bucket, set aside the bent roses, and filled the glasses with fizzy wine, handing one to Rose.

"And I have always loved you, Rose. Ain't that handy?" Oceanna spoke breathlessly.

They heaved sighs and giggled, touching, whispering, gazing, and drinking their wine enthusiastically. The driver took the long route to the studio, allowing the women extra time to connect while still ensuring they arrived on time, as ordered.

When the limousine stopped at the studio doors, Rose and Oceanna wore dreamy expressions, shared lingering looks, and smiled with the quiet satisfaction of lovers on their first date, feeling as vulnerable as virgins.

As they stepped out, Rose was unsteady. Oceanna pulled her close, hugging her fragile body tightly. Sparks of electricity seemed to jump between them with every step.

The studio was glamorous, flashy, and dimly lit. It radiated a vibrant, romantic atmosphere, filled with black boxes, panels of flickering lights, cameras on wheels, recording devices, and hanging microphones. The shiny black floors reflected the glow of expansive editing stations and recording monitors lit with red and green dots.

The station staff welcomed the women, offering them wine and seating them in the guest room while they waited for their spot. They sipped their drinks, sitting close, holding hands.

Finally, the stage was ready. Rose and Oceanna eased into their chairs as the news anchor entered, shook hands, and introduced herself. She briefly outlined the flow of the interview, complimented their appearance, and gave the high sign to the crew. Microphones were adjusted, and everything was set.

The anchor, young and energetic, began with sharp, probing questions, eager to uncover the details of the history they had experienced as it unfolded. She asked about their enduring friendship, how it had remained strong through calamity and distance, and how they had managed to communicate about their writing and the pact they had made to become authors.

Rose was congratulated on her brave recovery from cancer and asked how she had maintained her faith while riding the roller coaster of treatments.

The conversation turned to Jack Pontiac's Pulitzer Prize-winning photo. The anchor marveled at his uncanny ability to always be at the right place at the worst time throughout his career. She inquired about the controversy surrounding his use of grief to achieve personal gain and asked Oceanna if she had seen the life-sized photo now displayed in the Newseum—the final shot she had taken of her father, grinning and directing amid the raging calamity on his last day at Loves' farm.

The anchor then wondered what had driven Gretchen to kill her father and speculated on what had truly happened to her mother. She noted the bitter irony of the infamous Doctor Uhglee's demise—a sharp kick to the forehead by one of his mares in labor had knocked him unconscious, leaving him face-down in the steaming placenta. Helpless, he had drowned. Days later, his stiff, fly-covered body was found, a tragic end to his dubious legacy. Oceanna couldn't suppress the small smile that crept across her face as she recounted the story.

The discussion shifted to the process of writing. Oceanna shared the method she used to build a novel, one Rose had discovered in a mystery magazine. She described her astonishment at how the characters seemed to take over, writing the story themselves as though revealing a reality beyond the ordinary.

Rose admitted that she often forgot the characters weren't real and spoke of the strange feeling of betrayal she experienced when wanting to change the story against the characters' wishes. She shared how her dreams began to take over her sleep, pulling her into a world where reality and imagination intertwined, blending into something both profound and unsettling as her story unfolded.

"We are nearing the end of our time together, ladies," the news anchor said with a warm smile. "Your stories are truly fascinating. To finish our show, I'd like to ask you, Rose, the final question."

Rose had been gazing at Oceanna's face, captivated by the movement of her cheeks and the shape of her mouth as she spoke. Lost in a lover's fog—groggy, misty, and high—she was jolted back to attention when the questions turned to her.

"Rose, now that you have spent two years chasing the cure for cancer, enduring the trials of treatment, and writing a successful novel, what could possibly follow? After all this drama, what's next? What will your next adventure be?"

Rose blinked, suddenly realizing she needed to respond. She squeezed Oceanna's hand, feeling a wave of embarrassment and unpreparedness wash over her. She looked back at the anchor, whose red lips curled into a knowing chuckle.

Oceanna grinned, winked with one glassy green eye, and bit her lip.

"Uh-umm… well…?" Rose stammered.

*****